THE MYSTERY OF THE ABECEDARIAN ACADEMY

THE THREE INVESTIGATORS

IN

THE MYSTERY OF THE ABECEDARIAN ACADEMY

BY

ELIZABETH ARTHUR
& STEVEN BAUER

BASED ON CHARACTERS
CREATED BY ROBERT ARTHUR

Hollow Tree Press 2025

CONTENTS

1

A Message From Hector Sebastian

Bob Andrews glanced at his watch as he drummed his fingers on the glass-topped table. His best friends Pete Crenshaw and Jupiter Jones were probably already at the Jones Salvage Yard, working with the antique letterpress, printing copies of the new Three Investigators business card, while here he was, stuck on the small stone patio in the back yard of his house in Rocky Beach, waiting for his father's blueberry pancakes.

He'd agreed to have breakfast with his parents this morning, but this was taking forever. Come on, Dad, he thought. He loved his parents, but he was in a tearing hurry to join his friends – although, before he did, he'd promised Miss Bennett he'd put in two hours' work at the Rocky Beach Library. He'd been working at the library for years now, and normally he liked being there, but today was the first official day of the new investigative season!

The morning air was fresh and still cool, but every so often Bob thought he caught a whiff of something that smelled like smoke.

Through the silvery-gray leaves of eucalyptus, Bob squinted up at the deep blue of a clear California sky. Where was the smoke coming from? he wondered uneasily. California was a tinderbox, even in mid-June, and wildfires had been burning in the north, conflagrations that had roared across thousands of acres – blackening the sky with ash and plumes of smoke. So far the fires hadn't hit southern California.

The day before – the first day of summer vacation, with 8th grade behind them and high school not far ahead – Bob had been talking to Pete and Jupiter about the mysteries The Three Investigators hoped to solve this summer. Jupe had mentioned the fires and Pete had said – half-joking but also half-serious – that maybe there was a pyromaniac on the loose. Someone lighting the fires on purpose.

"No way," Bob had said.

"Don't be so certain, Bob," Jupiter had said. "The California Department of Forestry and Fire Protection thinks at least 10% of all fires are deliberately set."

"Who would do a thing like that?" Bob asked.

"Firebugs," Jupiter said, in his calm, reasonable voice. "They may appear relatively normal, but they lack the ability to empathize with other human beings, and they don't respond to punishment."

Jupiter had grown taller and slimmer over the last year, and he had even more information packed into his capacious brain.

"Do you remember the Dixie fire that burned almost 100,000 acres a few years ago?" he went on. "They arrested a former college professor who set a second set of fires *behind* the firefighters who rushed in to try to contain the first blaze."

"You're kidding," Pete said, an astonished look on his face. "That's totally crazy."

"Correct," Jupiter said. "They *are* crazy. That's why they call them pyro-*maniacs*. Most are male; most use matches or lighters; and most act out of boredom. They get an emotional rush from starting the fire. A guy named John Leonard Orr, who was a fire captain and an arson investigator, is suspected of having started over two thousand fires in California."

"A fire captain?" Bob said, amazed.

"An arson investigator?" Pete said, incredulous.

"He liked fires," Jupiter said. "And when he came across one he'd set himself, he could say for sure that it had been arson."

"Jeez," Pete had said. "How do you

know all this stuff?”

That was easy, Bob thought. Jupiter was a genius — though he hated it when someone called him that.

“I came across it in my reading,” Jupiter said blandly.

It seemed to Bob that Jupiter remembered everything he’d ever read. It had been Jupe’s idea for the three of them to form a detective firm, some years before. When they had, Jupiter’s Uncle Titus had given them an old mobile home trailer for them to use as their Headquarters. He’d bought the thing as salvage, but it had proven too badly damaged to sell, and by now it was hidden behind piles of carefully arranged junk that concealed its three secret entrances and a secret emergency exit from public view.

Jupiter had lived with Mathilda and Titus Jones ever since his parents had died when he was an infant, and these days Bob and Pete spent as much time at the Jones Salvage Yard as they spent at their own houses. When Jupiter’s aunt and uncle had started the Jones Salvage Yard — before Jupiter was even born — they’d simply called it a junk yard, but when Jupiter was still quite young, he’d convinced them to change the name, and with an attractive name and the ongoing interest in recycling, the place had been doing very well.

Bob smiled as he thought of Jupiter's aunt and uncle, two of the most eccentric people he'd ever met. Mathilda Jones, a big woman with a voice like a startled rooster, was red-cheeked and easily emotional, with a heart as big as the state of California, but she had a shrewd head for business and was the brains behind the Salvage Yard. Her husband Titus was an always-optimistic dreamer who lived for his trips out looking for things to buy.

Jupiter's aunt and uncle couldn't have been more different from Bob's parents. Bob's mother was a professor of evolutionary biology at nearby Reedmore College and Bob's father was a journalist for the Los Angeles *Sun*. Bob sometimes thought he, too, might be a journalist when he grew up. Malcolm Andrews was lanky and studious-looking and had red-blond hair – a reminder of his Scots/Viking ancestors. He'd moved to California from what he generally referred to as "the East" – by which he meant the eastern United States, where he'd grown up, gone to college, and studied journalism.

But Bob's mother's family really *was* from the East. Her parents had come to America from China in the 1960s. Bob's mother had been born in San Francisco. She'd met Bob's father when he was researching an article on the successive waves of Chinese immigration and he'd interviewed Bob's mother's parents about their escape from Maoist China. He'd fallen in love with Maxine, a budding scientist studying at UCLA, and they'd gotten married.

Bob was their only child, and somehow Bob felt closer to his father's forebears than his mother's. After all, he took after his father in lots of ways, including in his appearance. Although Bob's eyes looked a bit Asian, his hair was a light chestnut brown, and in the summer it was bleached blond by the sun. It seemed that Bob's grandfather had been from the part of China where people sometimes had blond hair, and although Maxine's hair was black, she'd told Bob she must have a recessive gene.

"Earth to Bob," Bob's father said as he put a plate of blueberry pancakes down in front of his son. "You were a million miles away."

At last! Bob thought as he stared up at his father. "Just remembering a conversation I had with Pete and Jupiter," he said. "By the way, do you smell smoke?"

"Smoke?" his father said. He paused, tilted his head back, and sniffed. "Now that you mention it, I do."

"Don't worry," Bob's mother said, bringing her own plate to the table. "It's probably old Mr. Townsend. He has a stone fireplace in his backyard that he sometimes burns paper and wood litter in. There's an ordinance against it just now, but the police don't have the heart to ticket him."

"I hope you're right," Bob's father said to her. "Was your conversation with Jupiter and Pete about the fires?" he asked Bob.

"In a way," Bob said. "But it was mostly about arson. Pete said that lightning strikes and high-voltage utility lines were bad enough without people running around starting fires. Then I said that everyone was so on edge these days that it would be easy to fool someone into leaving their house unlocked and unprotected by just knocking on their door, pointing into the distance, and yelling 'Fire!'"

"An acute observation," Malcolm Andrews said.

"That's what Jupiter said, too," said Bob. "He said that people are amazingly easy to frighten. That they rarely require solid evidence to back up assertions if their own safety is involved."

Bob stopped talking long enough to

shovel some pancakes into his mouth. "That sounds just like Jupiter," his mother said. "I've often wondered if he's going to grow up to be a scientist. So what are your plans for the summer?" she added. "Are you boys already working on a case?"

Bob's mouth was full of blueberry pancakes, but he nodded and chewed furiously.

"Not yet," he said. "But we're hoping to find something soon. I keep expecting I'll hear from Hector Sebastian. In fact, I e-mailed him last night asking him what was up."

The Three Investigators had met Hector Sebastian in the course of one of their early cases, and he'd been involved in their investigations ever since. He lived in a narrow canyon near Rocky Beach and was famous for writing mysteries in which modern technologies were used either to commit murders or to solve them.

For over two years now, he'd been helping them publicize their firm by writing introductions to their cases, but recently he'd said it might be time for Bob to start writing everything himself. In addition to his part-time job at the Rocky Beach Public Library, Bob worked full-time as Records and Research for The Three Investigators, and just last month he and

Pete and Jupe had decided it was time for the firm to have its own website. Hector Sebastian had approved.

"He's like a mystery magnet," Bob's mother said now. "Not only does he write mysteries, but he attracts them."

Bob laughed. His mother was right. Mr. Sebastian had often put them in touch with friends or acquaintances who wanted mysteries solved – people who needed help with something strange that had happened in their lives, but who would have felt silly hiring adult investigators for something that seemed so unimportant to anyone but them.

"Um hmm," he said, wiping his lips. He took a gulp of milk and swallowed. "And we want to go camping, too."

"Camping?" his mother asked, raising her eyebrows inquisitively. "Where?"

"Somewhere in the mountains," Bob said. "Among other things, we want to try out our new walkie-talkies. They're supposed to have a range of fifty miles."

Bob, Pete, and Jupiter had gotten flip-top cell phones when they'd turned thirteen – almost a year ago now. But before that, they'd always used walkie-talkies, and walkie-talkies still tended to work in a lot of places where cell phones didn't. Their new walkie-talkies had come with a handheld GPS, and though Bob was used to being the map reader when the three of them were out on cases, so far he liked what he'd seen of the new gadget and was eager to try it out.

He was also eager to get going. He stood up so suddenly that his chair skidded across the patio.

"Whoa, big guy," his father said.

"Sorry," said Bob. "But I have to run. I promised Miss Bennett I'd put in some time at the library, and the sooner I get there the sooner I can leave and get to the Salvage Yard."

He shoved what he needed into his backpack, fastened his bike helmet, and jumped on his bike. Despite his hurry, he decided to check out his mother's earlier deduction. Mr. Townsend lived two blocks away in a small bungalow. Sure enough, as Bob passed, he saw a plume of yellow-white smoke curling upwards from his small backyard. Some mysteries were easily solved!

Soon he was pedaling hard through the tree-lined streets of Rocky Beach. The town was far enough north of Los Angeles to have escaped the urban sprawl. It nestled comfortably between the range of coastal mountains and the Pacific Ocean. Rocky Beach was small and people were friendly. It was the only home Bob had ever known, and he liked it a lot.

As he slipped his bike into the bike rack at the Rocky Beach Public Library, it was 9:25. Bob went right to the Circulation Desk.

"Oh, Bob," Miss Bennett said. "Am I glad to see you. I've got a lot on my mind today."

Miss Bennett had been a fixture at the library ever since Bob could remember. Several years ago he'd broken his left leg in a bunch of places falling down a steep hillside he was climbing, and she'd gone out of her way to find books he might like when he'd spent over a month in bed. She was usually warm and friendly but she could be stern. Today, she mostly seemed flustered, and Bob wondered why.

"What do you want me to start with?" Bob asked.

"There are plenty of books to shelve," she said, "and I may need to call upon you later."

Bob loaded up a cart and took off for the stacks. Miss Bennett had been right – there were plenty of books to shelve. He was in the

Mystery section when he came across a book by Hector Sebastian and stopped to leaf through it.

Even though his mysteries were highly technical and technological, he'd once told Bob that Arthur Conan Doyle and Agatha Christie had created the modern mystery form − because they'd been the first writers to create fictional detectives who knew that if you want to solve a mystery, you need to pay attention to human nature.

Hector Sebastian had also pointed out that ordinary people could be extraordinary if they simply used their intelligence, their powers of observation, their deductive logic, and their common sense to see the truth that lay behind appearances. That was what Jupiter believed too, Bob thought.

Of course, Bob and Pete and Jupiter had also always liked gadgets that helped the investigative process along, but they'd never let gadgets get in the way of thinking hard.

There were a lot of books to put away, and as Bob pushed his − finally! − empty cart back toward the Circulation Desk, he glanced once again at his watch. It was already after eleven, and he'd be stopping work at 11:30. That should give him plenty of time to get to the Salvage Yard before noon.

Miss Bennett was behind the main desk, and she looked even more flustered than she had earlier.

"Bob?" she called to him. "I didn't know where you'd gotten to. I have to leave the library for a little while, and I need you to watch the desk."

"How long will you be?" Bob asked. "I have to – "

Miss Bennett swatted the air in front of her. "Only a minute," she said. "Now, you know how to check out books, of course, and besides, the library's almost empty."

"But – " Bob said.

"If you want to, you can use the computer," Miss Bennett said as she headed for the door.

Well, Bob thought. She'll only be a minute.

The library was quiet, and no one was anywhere near the Circulation Desk. To distract himself, Bob logged off the library system and opened his e-mail. Messages came flooding in, most of them junk. But as his eyes slid down the long row of senders, he was thrilled to see that he had a new message from Hector Sebastian. He was about to open it when he was startled by a voice so nasal and irritating it might have been a buzzing wasp.

Bob looked up to see E. Skinner Norris holding a bunch of books. Bob groaned. Skinny Norris was a jerk, plain and simple, and he seemed to spend every day honing his jerkiness. His nickname was perfect; he had a concave chest, arms like broomsticks, bristly blond hair the color of dried summer grass, and a protuberant Adam's apple. He was two years older than Jupiter, Pete, and Bob, and he'd made it his life's work to bother and insult The Three Investigators. Bob knew he was secretly jealous of them – of Jupiter most of all.

"Hello, Skinny," Bob said, looking him up and down. "When did you learn to read?"

"Ha, ha, very funny, Miss Andrews," Skinny said. "I'm just returning these for my mother. I wouldn't be caught dead with a book."

"I bet," Bob said. "And no decent book would be caught dead with you. Keep your voice down. This is a library."

Skinny dropped the books on the counter with a thud, making as much noise as possible.

"So what's up with you and your stupid friends?" Skinny asked. "How's old Jupiter McSherlock?"

Bob thought quickly. Maybe he'd have some fun with Skinny.

"Jupiter?" he said. "Oh, Jupiter's great! Over the last few weeks, his powers have been increasing by the day. Yesterday I saw him move a whole stack of reclaimed lumber with his mind."

Skinny's already narrow eyes narrowed further. He looked impressed but skeptical. "Maybe he'd better see if he can learn to move the three of you around with that big brain of his," he said. "Last I heard you were about to lose your wheels."

Unfortunately, Skinny was right. Several years ago, Jupiter had used his skill at deduction and analysis to ace a puzzle sponsored by the Rocky Beach Rent-'n'-Ride Auto Rental Company. By winning, he'd secured the use of a vintage Rolls-Royce sedan, complete with an English chauffeur. Through clever logic – and also with help from an English boy who appreciated their assistance in finding an Indian jewel called The Fiery Eye – Jupiter had managed to extend the initial thirty-day prize period again and again.

But now their use of the car had almost come to an end, and how The Three Investigators were going to get from place to place in the future was a mystery the boys were looking forward to solving. Although Bob had no use for Skinny, in one way he envied him a little. Skinny had his own car.

Bob wouldn't much miss the Rolls itself – it was comfortable, but it was also overly big, and gaudy, and so tricked out it was embarrassing – but he would certainly miss – they all would miss – its chauffeur, William Worthington. His reserve was mixed with affability and good humor, and he had helped The Three Investigators out of a lot of tight spots. He was lean, strong, very tall, quick-thinking, good-looking, and kind. All three boys were very fond of him.

"Thanks for your concern," Bob said to Skinny, "but we'll manage. Maybe you could lend us your sports car."

Skinny smirked. "Yeah, right," he said. "Like in a million billion years." He scratched his throat and his Adam's apple bobbed up and down. He picked up a stapler and put it down, then began playing with a paperclip.

"Don't you have somewhere better to be?" Bob asked. "Like preschool?"

"Actually, I'm hiding out," Skinny said, looking around exaggeratedly as though he'd been followed by spies. "I'm supposed to be helping my aunt and her daughter. They've just moved back to Rocky Beach, and my little cousin Mally-Wally isn't happy to be here, at all, at all. My parents want me to keep her company, but she's a total drag."

"Coming from you," Bob said, "that's quite a compliment."

Skinny looked at Bob with a combination of petulance and disgust.

"Well, Miss Andrews," he said. "Great seeing you. Don't let the bedbugs bite." He ran his hand through his hair, turned, and stalked out the door.

Bob looked around to make sure no one else was approaching and then clicked on Hector Sebastian's message. He'd thought Skinny would never leave. He stared at the black letters on the dazzling white screen with a growing sense of excitement.

"Dear Records and Research," it said. "Important news for the whole firm. Call me the next time The Three Investigators are at Headquarters. Hector Sebastian."

Wow! Bob thought. Important news! Just wait until the guys heard this!

He looked at his watch and his irritation grew. It was almost 11:45 and Miss Bennett was nowhere in sight. She'd said she'd only be a minute!

He went back to the computer to take his mind off his annoyance. He might as well do a bit of research about the best places to go camping in California. Maybe he and Pete and Jupiter could use their final days with Worthington and the Rolls to go farther afield than usual. He logged off his e-mail, called the library system up again, and started looking for interesting places to visit.

The first that popped up was the Gold Country, and for a while, Bob read about James Wilson Marshall discovering gold in the American River in 1848 and how the Gold Rush had started and enveloped the entire area. Even now, the Roaring Camp Mining Company offered gold panning, camping, and guided tours.

After that, Bob found himself reading about Yosemite Valley and John Muir – a Scottish-American naturalist who'd had a big influence on the preservation of wilderness in America. None of the boys had ever been to Yosemite, and as Bob studied the pictures of El Capitan and Half Dome, he thought it might be an excellent place to test their new walkie-talkies – and to use the elevation feature of their new GPS.

He closed the window and stared at the main entrance. It was almost noon. Where was Miss Bennett? He pounded his fist on the desk in frustration, then felt embarrassed as several library patrons looked at him. Aside from his own impatience, he knew that Pete would be worried by now. If anyone was ever late, Pete had a wild imagination for disaster.

At last, the library's front door opened and Miss Bennett hurried in, looking flushed. Bob got down off the stool he was perched on and went to meet her.

"I'm so sorry, Bob," she said. "I was at the post office and I ran into – "

"That's O.K., Miss Bennett," Bob said, "but I've got to get going. I'm late!"

He shrugged into his backpack and was out the door in a flash. He buckled his helmet as he ran, unlocked his bike from the bike rack, jumped on, and raced off toward the Jones Salvage Yard and his friends. He'd never need a GPS to find *them,* he thought!

2

A Chinese Talisman Against Demons

Pete Crenshaw shook his head in disbelief. For the last twenty minutes he'd been expecting Bob to show up at any moment, and he'd been keeping his eye on Green Gate One – a secret entrance in the fence surrounding the Jones Salvage Yard. It led directly into the outdoor workshop. There, Pete had been working hard on an antique letterpress Jupiter had found among the items brought home one day to the Salvage Yard by his uncle Titus.

With his uncle's permission, Jupiter had rebuilt it and moved it into the area in front of Headquarters. The outdoor workshop also had a band saw, a lathe, and a drill press – among other useful tools that Jupiter, Pete, and Bob had repaired when they had come in broken, and that they used when the need arose.

Today, though, Pete was the one who was mainly using the letterpress, while Jupiter was mainly sitting, working on a puzzle in a magazine his Uncle Titus had given him. He clearly felt he could do this safely because although the outdoor workshop wasn't quite as invisible to prying eyes as Headquarters was, at least it couldn't be seen from the Salvage Yard office where Jupiter's Aunt Mathilda worked.

Aunt Mathilda was a kind woman, Pete thought, but she had never really taken the firm of The Three Investigators as seriously as The Three Investigators themselves did, and if she saw the boys "just hanging around" as she called it, she always tried to put them to work. Pete didn't care.

In fact, he liked helping out, and especially in The Jones Salvage Yard – a truly fantastic place. After Jupiter had persuaded him to change the name from Jones's Junk Yard, his Uncle Titus had started to collect a lot of unusual items – old doors and signs, antique equipment and machines, leaded glass windows, fireplace mantels, plumbing fixtures, ceramic tiles, interesting old tools – as well as a pipe organ that had figured in The Three Investigators' very first case.

Now the Jones Salvage Yard was full to bursting with Uncle Titus's finds, gathered from all over southern California – some of them quite valuable, and all of them of interest to people looking to reclaim, refurbish, renovate, and rebuild.

Looking at Jupiter working on his puzzle,

Pete thought that although Jupiter and his uncle – Jupiter's father's much older half-brother – were in most ways very different, they had in common a fascination with puzzles and riddles and enigmas, and Jupiter thought he should complete any puzzles his uncle gave him. Pete understood this, but even so, he felt that, in *this* case, Jupiter should be helping print, dry, and stack The Three Investigators' new cards.

The cards said, as they always had:

THE THREE INVESTIGATORS
"We Investigate Anything"
???
First Investigator – Jupiter Jones
Second Investigator – Pete Crenshaw
Records and Research – Bob Andrews

What was different with this new batch was that at the bottom of the card was the number of the landline in Headquarters, the number of Bob Andrews's cellphone, and the brand-new website address of their firm.

Also, on the new cards the boys' names, and the question marks, were in three different colors – red, blue, and green, the colors of the chalk the boys sometimes used to leave secret signals for one another. Although using different colors for different words wouldn't be difficult on a computer, it was much more difficult – but also more substantial – on an old-fashioned printing press.

"Hey, Jupe," Pete finally called out. "These new cards are great! The unbleached card stock really makes the colors pop."

Jupiter looked up from his puzzle and squinted in the morning sunlight. In the last six months, he had grown a lot, and although in the past, he had sometimes looked somewhat stocky – and even pudgy – he was suddenly slimming down and shooting up.

That wasn't surprising, given his age, but what *was* a little surprising was that his hair, which had always been darker than Pete's, had now turned almost black – a real contrast to his blue-green eyes.

"Thanks, Pete," Jupiter said. "I think they bring the firm up to date."

"I can't imagine where Bob is," Pete said. "Do you know when your uncle's getting back, at least?"

Jupiter glanced at his watch. "It's almost noon," he said, "and Uncle Titus doesn't like to miss lunch. He left just after breakfast, and five hours should be plenty of time for him to check out the yard sales and estate sales he'd lined up. So, I'd expect him soon."

"Boy," Pete said. "I wonder what he'll bring back this time."

Pete never got tired of looking at the weird and wonderful stuff piled everywhere around him. Most of the objects were stored in wooden sheds, but there were so many that some had been stacked along the inside of the fence around the yard, which had a six-foot wooden overhang. One dedicated shed was a big empty open space – with a roof and poured concrete floor – which was used for unloading and sorting through Uncle Titus's latest haul.

The fence itself was solid wood and almost seven feet high. It ran around the entire circumference of the Salvage Yard and had only two official entrances. The front one held a set of gigantic gates that Jupiter's Uncle Titus had salvaged from a Hollywood estate, and the rear one opened onto a walkway that led to the house where Jupiter lived with his aunt and uncle.

On the outside, including in Jupiter's backyard, the fence had been painted along its entire length with murals crafted by local artists. The back had a depiction of the San Francisco Fire, and the front was covered with trees and flowers, green lakes and swans, and even an ocean scene.

The ocean scene showed a two-masted sailing ship foundering in a raging storm. There were two green boards in that scene which swung up when you pushed against the eye of a fish that was looking out of the water at the sinking ship, and Pete was almost certain that Bob would be pushing his bicycle through that entrance when he finally arrived.

They had another secret entrance to the Yard – Red Gate Rover, named after a little dog watching the San Francisco Fire – but that was on the other side of the Yard and led straight to the back of Headquarters. It was only used on rare occasions.

Where *was* Bob? Pete wondered. He'd said he was coming over right after work at the library, and Bob was never late. Never. He would love the new cards, but where *was* he? Had something happened? Had he been kidnapped? Fallen into a storm drain and broken his leg again? Been taken into outer space by aliens? Try as he might to remain cool-headed and logical, Pete was given to wild flights of fancy, and although he was a soccer and baseball player, and almost always took charge of the most difficult physical tasks facing The Three Investigators, he sometimes felt that his inside and his outside didn't really match.

Outside, he looked a lot like his father – who was also big and strong, and who had been working in the Hollywood movie business for many years, most recently as a construction manager on film sets – but inside there was a lot going on that surprised him.

For one thing, even two years after he and Bob and Jupiter had formed their own detective firm, Pete was still sometimes astonished that he was part of it.

The Three Investigators had actually evolved from a puzzle club that Jupiter had started when the boys were eight, and although Pete had pretended to Jupiter and Bob that he enjoyed solving puzzles and riddles as much as they did, he really didn't. He liked to *do* things – not think about them all that much first.

Also, even though his father was always explaining to Pete how easy it was to create an illusion – he knew this from his work in films – Pete's mother *believed* in illusions, a lot of the time. She was a fifth grade teacher at the Rocky Beach Elementary School – where Pete had just narrowly escaped being taught by his own mother! – but she believed in Tarot card reading and the I Ching and stuff like that.

Although she was descended from Spaniards who had come to California in the days when they were still building the Spanish missions, she was very broad-minded when it came to believing stuff that wasn't rational.

In fact, she had what she herself called "a big mystical streak," and Pete had learned a lot from her about what she called "alternative beliefs," which most people called superstitions. No single country had a corner on the superstition market, and Pete's mother was an equal opportunity believer – well-steeped in alternative beliefs from Ireland and China, as well as Spain and Mexico.

Although he didn't really believe in them, Pete somehow picked up these weird beliefs like lint. For example, he always threw salt over his left shoulder when he spilled some, never walked under ladders if he could help it, and had a rabbit's foot he sometimes carried in his pocket. He also knocked on wood, made wishes on wishbones, and crossed his fingers when he hoped for luck.

Pete's mother also believed in reincarnation, and just recently had told him that she was almost certain he was the reincarnated spirit of one of the Boy Soldiers who had died defending Mexico City's Chapultepec Castle from invading U.S. forces in the Battle of

Chapultepec, during the Mexican-American War. Pete didn't really believe this, either – although it was definitely flattering.

Still, Pete was anything but warlike, and by now he was old enough to have noticed that people always wanted to believe they were descended from (or the reincarnated spirits of) famous and courageous people – not unknown or cowardly ones.

In addition, Pete had a funny feeling that his mother wanted him to think he was a reincarnated hero partly because, in the *real* world, his father's parents had been hard-up farmers in Mexico before they came to America in the early 1960s, seeking a better life.

They'd been illiterate but savvy, and had changed their last name from Crespillo to Crenshaw when they ended up working as a maid and a gardener at a house in Los Angeles in Lafayette Square – an upscale housing development founded by a real estate developer named George Lafayette Crenshaw.

As far as Pete could understand, they'd changed their surname to help ensure their children got a good education and became what his grandparents called "true Americans." But although his father and uncles and aunts *had* gotten a good education in the United

States – and had, in fact, become completely American – eventually they'd realized their parents hadn't *needed* to change their name, and Pete's father had considered changing his name back to Crespillo.

However, he hadn't, in the end. He was who he was, he felt – a man named Martín Crenshaw.

As for Pete, he was who he was, too, he thought – one of The Three Investigators, as well as his parents' son.

He'd just finished the last of the hundred cards he'd printed and had begun to clean the ink from the handset type when he heard, coming closer, the familiar roar of the Salvage Yard's biggest truck.

"Here he comes," yelled Pete. Hurriedly he wiped his hands and managed to smear ink all over his fingers. He dropped the cloth and joined Jupiter, who now stood near the large filigreed wrought-iron gates that framed the central entrance to the Salvage Yard.

The old truck pulled in, Uncle Titus waving cheerfully, with the Salvage Yard's two Norwegian carpenters, Leif and Magnus Haldorsson, balancing in the truck bed among the day's finds.

Since the Salvage Yard had a lot of reclaimed lumber for sale, when Hans and Konrad – also brothers, originally from Bavaria – who had worked for Uncle Titus and Aunt Mathilda, driving trucks and hauling heavy goods around, had both gotten married and started new jobs, Aunt Mathilda had had the idea to hire replacements who would not only be able to help Uncle Titus, but would also be on-site carpenters, available to anyone who came into the Salvage Yard looking for a specially sized door or window or piece of furniture.

Uncle Titus jumped out as Leif and Magnus climbed down.

"Boys!" he yelled. "Wait 'til you see what I found! But before we start unloading – " He crossed his arms on his chest and looked at Jupiter.

"While I was driving, I thought of a puzzle for you. If the day after tomorrow comes three days after Wednesday, then what was the day before yesterday?"

Pete's head spun. Uncle Titus was always doing this, and, what was worse, Jupiter was always up to the challenge. Jupiter smiled and pinched his lower lip between his thumb and forefinger – the sign that he was thinking hard.

"Let's see," he said. "Three days after Wednesday is Saturday. If that's the day after tomorrow, then today must be Thursday. And in that case, the day before yesterday has to be Tuesday."

Uncle Titus roared with appreciation and smacked his hands together. "That's my boy!" he said. "Right on the money. Now let's get to work."

He put his hands on Pete's and Jupiter's shoulders and shepherded them toward the back of the truck. Leif and Magnus had already dropped the tailgate and removed the blue tarpaulin that had covered the new salvage.

"What's that all over your fingers, Pete?" Uncle Titus asked.

Pete stared down at his hands in surprise. "It's ink from the letterpress."

"Then you'd better stand back and let the rest of us unload," Uncle Titus said.

"But it's already dry!" Pete said.

"Let's not take chances," Uncle Titus said.

Pete groaned in frustration. Crestfallen, he stepped back and let the others begin the work as Jupiter's Aunt Mathilda joined them. She was a large woman, but a fast thinker like

her husband – if not given to all his enthusi-
asms. She had a preference for items she could
sell.

"Well, Titus," she said, her hands on her
hips. "What have we here?"

"Look at this, Mathilda," Uncle Titus
said. There was a stained glass window of twin-
ing vines with red berries which Aunt Mathilda
very much admired, an old oak armoire, a set
of armor that might or might not have been
real (Aunt Mathilda shook her head doubtfully),
an antique cash register with some of the keys
missing, and an ugly square box with a curved
gray screen.

"Titus?" Aunt Mathilda said incredulously. "What are we going to do with a 1960s
black and white TV?"

"Never mind that," Uncle Titus said.
"What do you make of these?"

Jupiter helped his uncle unwrap what
looked to be a stack of pictures, each about
three feet wide by four feet high, printed on
thin sheets of shiny metal.

"These are great, Uncle Titus," Jupiter
said.

"Wow!" Pete said. "What are they?"

There were eight of them, each different,
each a riot of color and form, and each a mys-

tery to Pete.

The one that caught his attention had, on its top, a very old Chinese man wearing a green crown and holding a fat green sword. He was swathed in a saffron robe on which were three circles. In each circle were three black lines, some of them broken in the middle – and looking very much like the top or bottom half of the symbols his mother consulted nearly every day in her copy of the I Ching.

The man's eyebrows slanted up, his mustache slanted down, and his hair and beard whooshed away from his face as if every follicle was electrified. Below him, on the bottom half of the panel, was a configuration of thick black lines, straight and curved, beautifully arranged but conveying no meaning to Pete – though they didn't look like regular Chinese characters.

"Boys," Uncle Titus said proudly. "These are Chinese talismans. The one that fascinates Pete is a Chinese talisman against demons."

"Demons!" Pete said. "Whoa!" Though Pete knew there was no such thing as a demon – really, there wasn't, right? –. as Pete looked at the Chinese talisman, he thought two things. First, he wished it were a bit smaller so that he could carry it in his pocket. And second, that

Bob would be as crazy about these talismans as he was.

"Where did you get these, Uncle Titus?" Jupiter asked.

"You know, that's the strangest thing. They were at a yard sale, tucked out of sight, one right on top of the other. The man who sold them said he found them in the attic of the house he bought. He seemed to think they were worthless and gave me all eight for twenty dollars. I think they're magnificent, and I don't even know if I want to sell them."

"I think we should hang them on a wire where you can see them through the Salvage Yard's gates," Jupiter said. "Pete and I can use the drill press to punch holes in the corners and we can string all eight of them up across the entrance to the office."

"Great idea," Uncle Titus said. "And let's put the new suit of armor by the gate. We can wire its arm so it points to the talismans."

"They're so colorful," Pete said, "and waving in the wind, they'll catch everyone's attention. What are the other ones?"

"Well," Uncle Titus said. "As far as I can remember, there's a talisman to attract prosperity, and one to ward off illness, and one to bring happiness."

"That's what we want," Pete said. "Prosperity, health, and happiness. And no demons!"

"Now, that's a good day's work," Aunt Mathilda said, "and I'll be the talisman against hunger. Is anyone ready for lunch?"

"My dear," Uncle Titus said. "You read my mind."

"That's not so hard to do," Aunt Mathilda said. "Boys?"

Jupiter looked at Pete, who shook his head. "No, thanks, Aunt Mathilda," Jupiter said. "We need to wait for Bob. He must have been held up at the library. While we're waiting, we can get started on these talismans."

"All right," Aunt Mathilda said. "I'll leave some sandwiches in the fridge." She walked off toward the house.

"Now, be careful with those," Uncle Titus warned. "Don't drill the holes too close to the corners or the metal might split."

Leif and Magnus hopped in the truck and Uncle Titus drove it slowly to the back of the Yard and parked it in front of the open shed where they did their unloading and sorting. Pete and Jupiter put the talismans into a cart and rolled it to their outdoor workshop.

"After we hang these up," Pete said,

"there's not a person in southern California who'll be able to resist coming in."

"That's just what I thought," Jupiter said. He examined the metal on which the talismans had been printed. "Brushed aluminum," he said. "About an eighth of an inch thick. That will be easy work for the drill press." He turned to Pete. "Would you hand me a 3 millimeter bit? That should make a hole plenty big enough to string the wire through."

Pete rummaged in the box that held the bits and found the one Jupiter had asked for. Jupiter opened the chock, inserted the bit, and tightened.

"You know," he said, "every time I use tools out here in the workshop, I think about what a really great thing your father did."

"You mean that fight over shop class?" Pete asked.

The year before, the school board had voted to eliminate all shop and woodworking classes from the curriculum, claiming financial difficulties. Pete's father, who was an expert at construction, knew the importance of that sort of education for all boys, but especially for those who wouldn't go on to college. He'd asked Bob's father for help, and although the men didn't have a lot in common, they united in a common cause.

Mr. Andrews wrote editorial after editorial for the Rocky Beach *Herald* about different modes of education and the importance of vocational training, the boys printed up hundreds of flyers on the letterpress, and Pete's father recruited an army of volunteers to go door-to-door to convince the townspeople to save the program.

"Yes," Jupiter said. "The way your father and Bob's father worked together to save the day. All the world's great inventors started with practical knowledge and skills. We need that today as much as we ever did."

Pete knew that Jupiter had recently been reading a book about inventors, with sections on Johannes Gutenberg and Nikola Tesla and Samuel Morse and Alexander Graham Bell and Thomas Edison.

In fact, just that morning, when they were setting up the printing press, Jupiter had pointed out that when Johannes Gutenberg invented movable type, he had changed the world forever, in the original "information revolution."

Even so, Pete was startled by Jupiter's praise of his father. He blushed as he watched Jupe put on his safety goggles. Jupe was about to plug in the machine when Green Gate One flipped open with a bang and Bob Andrews finally pushed his bike through.

"Bob!" Pete yelled. "Am I glad to see you! Of all days for you to be late!"

"Sorry, guys," Bob said. He filled them in quickly on Miss Bennett and Skinny Norris and was about to go on when Pete interrupted him.

"Skinny!" Pete said. "I thought we'd be free of him now that's school's out. Boy, I feel sorry for that cousin of his. Can you imagine having Skinny assigned to keep you company? Look what Jupiter's uncle brought back. Old Chinese good luck charms!"

He stood two of the prints up, next to each other, so that Bob could get the full effect. "Aren't they great? This is my favorite – it keeps demons away."

Bob crossed his arms and looked at the prints with an expression that Pete could only call skeptical.

"What?" Pete said. "You don't like them? I thought you'd be crazy about them."

"You know how logical my mother is," Bob said. "And even if she weren't, I doubt I'd be tempted to believe in ancient Chinese superstitions."

"I didn't mean you'd *believe* in them. I just thought you'd like them," Pete said.

"I do think they're interesting-looking," Bob admitted. "Anyway, I didn't tell you the most important thing. When I was at the library, I got an e-mail from Hector Sebastian. He wanted us to call him as soon as we were all together at Headquarters."

Jupiter took off his safety goggles, his eyes alight. "Why didn't you tell us right away?"

"Well, I tried to but —"

"Come on!" Jupiter said. He put down the talisman he was holding, made sure the power tools were all turned off, then started to sprint in the direction of Easy Three, Bob and Pete hot on his heels.

3

An Assemblage At Headquarters

Fifteen minutes later, the boys were finally sitting inside the old mobile home trailer, and Jupiter was happy to be there at last. They'd been delayed in their arrival because – as Jupiter had eventually deduced – when Pete had come in earlier in the day, he'd emerged with his hands full of card stock and had forgotten to put the key to Easy Three back in the metal box where it belonged after the door had locked behind him.

Easy Three was a big oak door – still on its hinges and in its frame – that blocked a clear view of Headquarters. Next to the door, as a joke, was a dented metal sign that read "Office," with a finger pointing to the entrance. A big metal key, concealed in a rusty metal box in a barrel of other rusty metal, opened the lock – after which a short passageway led to the original side door of the mobile home trailer.

Because Easy Three really *was* an easy entrance, when the boys first started their firm, they'd used it only on rare occasions. In those days, Jupiter reflected, the boys had been smaller (and younger) and had gotten a kick out of clambering into Headquarters through Tunnel Two – a length of corrugated pipe hidden behind the printing press and an old metal grate.

The pipe led to a trapdoor in the floor of Headquarters, but although the boys had long ago put down carpeting to save their knees, all three of them had grown too tall to want to wiggle through the pipe any longer – and the trapdoor was a special kind of torture.

For these reasons, they almost never used Tunnel Two any more – though Jupiter sometimes used a panel at the back of the mobile home that was accessed from Red Gate Rover. Since Emergency One – an escape hatch in the roof of the mobile home that led directly to an old kid's slide – only opened from the inside, Easy Three was the entrance they almost always used now.

Jupiter had found the missing key by asking Pete to review everything he'd done when he'd gone into Headquarters earlier to get more card stock. Pete had told Jupiter that he'd dropped some of the paper onto an old apple press when he'd been coming out – at which Jupiter deduced that Pete had also had the key in his hands when he dropped the stock and bent down to pick it up. Shortly afterwards, Jupiter had discovered the key inside the apple press, and now he and his two best friends were sitting comfortably around the phone in Headquarters, preparing to call Hector Sebastian.

Over the years, Headquarters had gotten more and more crammed with stuff. On the floor in the corner, under a layer of dust, was an old Olympia typewriter, and on the desk sat an aging computer with a monitor, a run-down printer, a rather large magnifying glass, a sub-station of the Salvage Yard's intercom that connected Headquarters to Aunt Mathilda's office, and an old-fashioned phone Jupiter had salvaged when his uncle brought it back in a box of junk.

The walls had built-in shelves piled high with supplies – including various telephone directories, outdated copies of the Yellow Pages, a dictionary, and other reference books – while a small gray, dented filing cabinet was filled to bursting with research and notes from old cases. From the ceiling hung a single shaded light bulb that cast a dim glow over everything, and as Bob cleared an open space on the desk on which to set his backpack, Jupiter made a mental note to spend an afternoon with his friends cleaning the place out.

Not today, though. Now that they were finally inside Headquarters, Jupiter could hardly wait to hear Hector Sebastian's news. In the past, this had almost always led to a case for The Three Investigators, and with summer just starting, Jupiter was anxious for a new challenge. He settled himself in a broken-down swivel desk chair behind the desk – one end of which had been scorched in a fire – while Pete and Bob sat in folding chairs opposite him.

The boys had Hector Sebastian's cell-phone number on speed-dial, and Jupiter punched the code and the speakerphone button so all three of them could hear and talk.

On the third ring, the phone was picked up, and Jupiter heard the deep rich plummy tones he knew so well.

"Hector Sebastian," the voice said.

"Mr. Sebastian. It's Jupiter Jones."

"Jupiter!" Mr. Sebastian said. "You got my message. Are Pete and Bob with you?"

"We're here," Bob said.

"Hi, Mr. Sebastian," said Pete.

"You have important news?" Jupiter asked.

"Yes," Hector Sebastian said. "I do. Important to me and important to you. In fact there are two things I want to tell you, one quite short and the other quite complicated."

A flash of static came over the speaker. Hector Sebastian's voice flickered and broke up, but then came back stronger.

"Hello?" he said. "Hello?"

"We're still here," Jupiter assured him. "We lost you for a moment."

"I'm driving in one of the canyons south of you," Mr. Sebastian said, "and coverage is iffy. Now, as I was saying. I think you'll quite like the complicated news, but I'm afraid you might not be happy about the simple bit.

"As I've told you, I'm tired of the mysteries I've been writing. I want to get back to basics, set my mysteries in the past – in fact, the Old West. Which is why I've decided to move to Wyoming – "

"Move to Wyoming!" Pete shouted.

" – and I've rented a house on a ranch in – "

At that moment, the phone went dead.

Jupiter sat and stared at the phone as if he could will it back to life, while Pete jumped from his chair in frustration and smacked his palms together.

"Wyoming?" Pete said again. "What's in Wyoming? I'm not even sure I know where it is." Pete liked to exaggerate, but in this case, Jupiter thought it was possible he meant what he said. Pete had a remarkable sense of direction but had never been all that good with maps. Maps were an abstract representation of reality, and a sense of direction was immediate and concrete.

"This is bad news," Jupiter said, "but we don't know how long he'll be gone. And he said we would like the rest of what he had to tell us."

Bob looked extremely gloomy. "What will we do without him?" he said. "He wrote up all our cases and gave us publicity, and introduced us to his friends – "

"Yeah," Pete said. "And this is on top of just about running out of time on the Rolls, which means we've got to say goodbye to Worthington, too."

That was something Jupiter had tried not to think about. From the very beginning – when Worthington had rescued him and Pete after they'd been tied up in the dungeon of Terror Castle, on their very first case – he'd had a special feeling for the chauffeur. Worthington had long since stopped being a driver and had become a sort of friend, and if Jupiter didn't exactly confide his feelings to him – well, that was because he didn't exactly confide his feelings to anybody. But Worthington was not only dependable, courageous, good-humored, private, and unflappable, but he took Jupiter utterly seriously.

Jupiter remembered well the first time the Rolls had pulled up to the Salvage Yard and Worthington had jumped out. He was over six feet tall and he'd stood at attention, holding his chauffeur's cap, the creases in his trousers as sharp as knives. He'd almost looked like a chauffeur in a movie, and Jupiter had been embarrassed when Worthington addressed him as "Master Jones."

Over time, to Jupiter's gratification, Worthington had relaxed. He'd spent time just talking with the boys and had eventually admitted that the reason he'd looked to Jupiter like a movie chauffeur might have been because when he'd come to California from England, he'd hoped to make it in the film world, and he'd been cast as a chauffeur (and also as a butler) in a number of second-string movies.

He was not just unusually tall, but also unusually handsome – and in a rather unusual way – and although he had grown up in rural

Cornwall and had no experience in cities, he'd had a passion for movies when he was growing up and had learned to speak with what in England was called a "posh" accent. Unfortunately, his speech and exotic good looks had not been enough to give him a full-time career in the movies, and after a director who'd directed him as a butler actually *hired* him as one, Worthington had rethought his career choice.

After all, he realized, he'd been paid more to be a real butler than to act as one. Worthington hadn't wanted to be a butler, but he'd thought being a driver might suit him nicely, so he'd taken a professional driving course and set out to be the best *real* British chauffeur in southern California.

To Jupiter, Worthington's life history seemed to give them a special bond, because when Jupiter was very young, he himself had been cast in a short-lived comical television series. In *his* case, it had given him a dislike of being laughed at, and a determination to be taken seriously, and if he had been the kind of person who held grudges, he might have never forgiven his Aunt Mathilda – whose idea it had been.

Instead, he had long ago put it behind him – although, even now, he sometimes drew on his early experience to act stupider than he really was. He had found it useful to have the skills to let his face grow slack and his eyes grow dull when he was dealing with someone he suspected was trying to deceive him.

This had been easier when he was younger and heavier – less distinctively himself – but even now that he was suddenly getting taller and leaner, he could still do it when he needed to, and when he did, Worthington always noticed and complimented him.

"Why isn't Mr. Sebastian calling back?" Bob asked.

"His phone is being blocked by the canyon," Jupiter said. "I'm sure he'll call as soon as he can."

At that exact moment, the phone rang.

"Three Investigators' Headquarters," Jupiter said. "Jupiter Jones speaking."

"Jupiter, it's Hector Sebastian. A thousand apologies for the interruption."

"Mr. Sebastian?" Pete blurted out. "Why do you have to move to Wyoming? Can't you just live here and write about the Old West?"

"Pete," Mr. Sebastian said. "Obviously you have never been to Wyoming."

"You can say that again," Pete said.

"Though my father almost went there once to work on a movie being filmed in some sort of Wild West town."

"It's another world," Mr. Sebastian said. "Sagebrush deserts and red rock cliffs, pristine rivers and elk and wolves and moose."

"Wolves?" said Pete. "Really?"

"Really. Your father would have loved it. And I think I've heard of that Wild West town. It's on a movie ranch called the Malachi Wagner Movie Ranch. It's on the west side of the Wind River Mountains," Hector Sebastian said. "I've found a house to rent on a dude ranch – well, they call them guest ranches now – near Dubois, on the other side. Now, let me finish before we get disconnected again. I want you boys to come to my house early tomorrow afternoon. I have two things to give you."

Jupiter smiled with satisfaction. One of them was surely a new case.

Hector Sebastian cleared his throat. "I said you wouldn't like the first thing I had to tell you, and I was right. But I'm sure you'll like this one."

"Should I take notes, Mr. Sebastian?" Bob asked."

"No need, Bob. Plenty of time for that. Just listen closely."

All three boys leaned forward instinctively.

"I have an old friend," Hector Sebastian went on. "Her name is Isabella Chang. She's in her mid-80s, but she's still as energetic as a colt and sharp as a good cheddar. I've told her about you boys and she's interested in speaking with you."

Jupiter could see that his friends were as intent on the details as he was.

"Isabella taught history to 9th and 10th graders, and since she retired, she's turned her hand to writing books – mostly about some aspect of California history. Her new book is a bit different in that it ties together that history with her family history."

"I take it from her name that your friend is Chinese," Jupiter said.

"Yes," Hector Sebastian said. "But other things as well. Like most Americans, she's a product of the melting pot – though it's true that the ancestor she's now interested in was Chinese. Well, both Chinese and Irish. She's trying to find out about a man named Li Chang whose Irish mother and Chinese father met and married during the Gold Rush."

"Wow," Bob said. "I was just reading about the Gold Country."

"Li was educated in a one-room school-house in a hamlet near the town of Cool. And that's the tie-in. Because Isabella's book is about Abecedarian Academies."

"A B C what?" Bob asked.

"That's what Isabella calls one-room schoolhouses. "Abecedarian" as an adjective means either "arranged alphabetically" or "rudimentary and elementary," but A-B-C-darians were the youngest students in the typical one-room schools of 19th-century America."

"What a great word!" Bob said. "And because of the way it starts, I doubt I'll ever forget it."

Jupiter wanted to hear more about the case. "But how can we help your friend?" he asked.

"As I said, Isabella is getting older, and though she's spry in many ways, her eyesight isn't what it was. She can't read and research as well as she used to, and she isn't able to use computers. Since she knows a lot of genealogical research is appearing online these days, she's looking for help in finding out more about Li. Do you think you boys could help?"

Jupiter was, if truth be told, a little disappointed. Researching genealogical information on the Internet wasn't likely to be as challenging or exciting as some of their past cases had been. But then again, who could tell? The most complex mysteries often began quite quietly, and, after all, the motto of The Three Investigators was *We Investigate Anything*.

"She'll tell you more if you can come to my house tomorrow. It seems that Li's father was murdered."

"Murdered!" Pete said. "Yikes!"

Already, Jupiter thought, things were getting more interesting. Not that he approved of murder, of course. But when there *were* murders, there were also strong emotions, and strong emotions were frequently at the heart of mysteries.

"There's more to it than that, of course. Gold might come into it somewhere. So will you come?" Hector Sebastian asked. "Early afternoon? About 2:00 or 2:30?"

"We'll be there," Jupiter said. "That is, if Pete and Bob can make it." Both the other boys nodded feverishly, so Jupiter continued. "It's all set, Mr. Sebastian. I'll call for the Rolls and Worthington. It'll be good to see you, and we look forward to meeting your friend."

"Great!" Hector Sebastian said. "See

you tomorrow!" He ended the call, and the line went dead.

"I was waiting for something to come our way," Jupiter said as he punched off the speakerphone.

"Gold!" Pete said. "And murder!"

"Still, I wish Mr. Sebastian wasn't moving away," Bob said, looking dejected.

"He isn't going to Mars," Jupiter said. "We can always call him or e-mail him. And besides, I have a hunch that we don't need Mr. Sebastian's help as much as we used to."

"What do you mean?" Bob asked.

"Yeah," Pete said. "Mr. Sebastian is a great guy and we'll miss him a lot. He's always fun to talk to. But Jupe's right, Bob. After all, you're the one who's been writing up all the notes on our cases practically forever. You're the one who puts everything in order so it makes sense."

"And now that The Three Investigators have a website," Jupiter said, "all you have to do is type up your notes and post them with a catchy title."

"You mean like a blog?" Bob asked.

Jupiter nodded. "You know I don't like that word, but yes, that's what I mean."

Bob looked doubtful, but Jupiter had

every confidence in his friend. Bob had been getting better and better as a writer and Jupiter was sure that, without anything to hold him back, he'd become a first-rate chronicler of The Three Investigators.

Although Jupiter changed his mind every few months about where his own talents might be best applied when he was an adult, he had long thought that Bob had been born to set his thoughts on paper.

"You said that you were just reading about the Gold Country?" he asked him.

"That, and Yosemite," Bob replied. "I started by researching places we might go camping this summer, but I ended up reading about John Muir, the Scottish-American naturalist whose writing helped get Yosemite set aside as a National Park."

"Yosemite!" Pete said. "What an idea! Maybe we could make it a great last trip with Worthington. Shouldn't you call the Rent-'n'-Ride, Jupe?"

Jupiter nodded and dialed the Rent-'n'-Ride's number while Pete and Bob kept talking. As he held for first one person and then another, he wasn't really listening to Bob and Pete.

Although in the background he could

hear Bob giving Pete a lot of details about Yosemite and John Muir, he found himself thinking about Worthington and Hector Sebastian and the new case. He felt oddly unsettled by the realization that two adults who had figured so prominently in the success of The Three Investigators over the past two years would soon be exiting their lives – at least for a while in the case of Hector Sebastian, and maybe forever in the case of Worthington.

In fact, although his first reaction to a case which involved researching a distant ancestor had been distinctly unenthusiastic, the more Jupiter thought about it, the more he understood why people frequently, at some point in their lives, got interested in the particular history of their individual families. America had always been a great place for immigrants from other countries to build new lives, but it had also been so big that people could lose track of both their ancestors and their living relatives.

Also, while Pete had a lot of cousins and aunts and uncles, aside from his Uncle Titus, Jupiter had no living blood relatives that he knew of. His great-great-great-great grandfather Jones had been a Welsh coal miner who had come to California about ten years after the California Gold Rush started, and had gotten a job working as a hard-rock miner in the Empire Mine near Grass Valley.

That first Jones had married and had children, but unfortunately, a number of his descendants had died in the terrible flu epidemic of 1918, and a number more had died in the Second World War. After that, one thing and another had happened to the Jones family to reduce its numbers, so that by the time Titus (and, later, Titus's half-brother Claudius) had been born, their particular branch of the Welsh-derived Jones family had almost died out.

Of course, Jupiter might have unknown aunts and uncles and cousins on the other side of his family — his mother's side. There was a mystery about Jupiter's mother, really. The only information his Uncle Titus had ever given Jupiter was that her family had been Serbian, and that she'd spoken the Serbian language; that she and Jupiter's father had met in Canada; and that Jupiter's parents had gotten married, had a baby, and been killed in a car crash before Uncle Titus and Aunt Mathilda had ever had a chance to meet Jupiter's mother.

Since Uncle Titus had been the only living relative of *either* of Jupiter's parents the Canadian government could track down, Canadian government officials had delivered the baby Jupiter to his Uncle Titus and Aunt Mathilda in a hand-off ceremony in the Los Angeles Canadian Consulate General.

As Jupiter sat thinking about this history and waiting to get through to the right person at the Rent-'n'-Ride, he wondered why, up to now, he had never tried to learn much about Serbia, or Serbian history. All he really knew about Serbia was that it had been the country in which the First World War had been triggered when the heir to the Austro-Hungarian throne had been assassinated in the city of Sarajevo. The assassin had worked for a Serbian secret society called the Black Hand.

Jupiter had always liked the name "the Black Hand" – which seemed like something straight out of the stories written by Arthur Conan Doyle – and for a moment, he wondered idly if any of his Serbian relatives had ever known anyone in the society. However, at that point, Jupiter was finally connected to the proper party at the Rent-'n'-Ride, and he was able to confirm that Worthington and the Rolls would be available the following day at 1:00.

"It's on!" he said to Pete and Bob. "Let's hope this case turns into something big!"

4

Heading For Dial Canyon

At half-past noon the next day, Bob, freshly scrubbed and neatly dressed, stood at the entrance to the Salvage Yard. The suit of armor Mr. Jones had brought back the day before was next to him, its visor shut, its arm wired so that its chain-mail-gloved hand pointed jauntily upward.

"He'll be like the host at a party," Pete had said. "Welcoming everybody."

Pete now stood at the top of a stepladder, positioning the last of the eight Chinese talismans on a wire stretched across the Salvage Yard in front of the office's front porch. That office – a little western-style cabin, really – stood about twenty feet behind the center of the gates.

"Be careful," Bob said.

Pete grinned at him. "I'm always careful."

Jupiter stood about ten feet back, directing operations.

"Just a bit more to the right," he said. Pete did as Jupe had suggested, and Jupiter nodded in satisfaction. "I'd say that's just about perfect," he said.

Bob had to agree. The aluminum panels swayed in the breeze as Pete clambered down. They glinted in the sunlight, and since they were mainly bright yellow, to say that they were eye-catching was an understatement.

They were impressive, and Bob was getting to like them almost as much as Pete had hoped – though he wasn't letting on. They were splendid decorations, calling cards, advertisements. Jupe and Pete had been right. No one could possibly drive down the road in front of the yard without catching sight of them right inside the gates.

Bob had arrived that morning right after breakfast, still somewhat unhappy about the fact that Hector Sebastian was moving to Wyoming, and not as certain as Jupiter and Pete that he'd be able to use the firm's new website to write up The Three Investigators' cases properly.

For one thing, there were an awful lot of websites out there – although only one Hector Sebastian – and, for another, Bob wasn't certain he could find a way to keep readers reading at a time when people's attention spans seemed to be getting shorter and shorter.

Still, after joining Pete and Jupiter in the workshop and working in the sunshine for a while, he'd come to feel more hopeful. The three boys had labored with the drill press to position holes in the upper corners of the panels. Then, working together, with two stepladders and a spool of thin wire, they'd managed to string the panels and get them hung. They'd done a great job, Bob thought. The Rolls was due to arrive sometime before one o'clock. Then they'd be off to Dial Canyon and the home of Hector Sebastian.

In the meantime, Jupiter had announced that he planned to read the section of his book about inventors that dealt with the Serbian-American inventor Nikola Tesla. Jupe took the book off to the outdoor workshop – out of sight of the main gates – while Bob settled in a lawn chair from which he could see the Rolls when it arrived.

As he doodled in his notebook, Bob was thinking about the word "abecedarian" and something Mr. Sebastian had once told Bob about Agatha Christie's book *The A.B.C. Murders*. He had said that the first time he'd read it – when he was still a boy – it had made him think about how the human mind loves to find patterns, and that if you want to capture someone else's imagination, you have to give them a pattern – like the pattern of alphabetical murders.

This had struck Bob as true, and now he wondered whether he could find a way to pattern The Three Investigators' cases when the time came to write them up on their blog. Giving them catchy titles, as Jupiter had suggested, would certainly help, he thought.

Bob was actually a little nervous about the upcoming visit – in part because he'd be saying goodbye to Mr. Sebastian, at least for a while, and in part because he was worried Isabella Chang would expect him to know more than he actually *did* know about the role Chinese immigration had played in the California Gold Rush.

Although he was generally very thorough, and both his friends and his parents thought him very dependable, in this case, he'd failed to do his homework, and he wished he'd brought his laptop so he could log onto the Salvage Yard's Wi-Fi and at least find out *something*.

Since all he had with him was a notebook, a pen, and the GPS, he was watching Pete pace restlessly back and forth around the yard when a girl on a bicycle rolled to a stop in front of the main gates.

The first thing Bob noticed was that she wasn't wearing a helmet; she ran both hands through her hair, then gripped her head as she stared – apparently incredulously – at the suit of armor. After that she dismounted, leaned her bike against the iron gate, and walked up to the armor to examine it more closely.

Though the girl was about his age, and Rocky Beach was a smallish town, Bob was sure he'd never seen her before. She was tall for her age, and slender, with slightly wavy shoulder-length red hair, and bangs cut short and straight above her eyebrows. She was wearing what looked to Bob like a kilt turned into shorts.

Bob was about to get up and go introduce himself when Pete zoomed in, a wide grin on his face.

"Hi," he said. "Can I help you?"

The girl looked at him coolly. "Are you responsible for this armor?" she asked. She had a noticeable accent, sort of English but different. It could be Scottish, Bob thought.

"I – ," Pete began, but the girl ran right over whatever he planned to say.

"In the old days, soldiers wore armor to keep from getting maimed or killed in battle, and even though this armor's clearly fake, I don't see why you want to treat it disrespectfully," she said.

"Disrespectfully?" Pete yelped.

Bob's interest was piqued. Pete was good-looking – tall and muscular, with coarse brown hair, brown eyes, high cheekbones, and a wide grin – and most girls their age fell under his spell quite easily. This one might prove a harder sell.

"I respect that armor a lot," Pete added. "A *lot*. We were just trying to let everyone know how great the Jones Salvage Yard is. If you like stuff, you've come to the right place. We don't usually put armor out front. Just today."

"Why today?" the girl asked.

"Because we just hung up those metal signs," Pete said, pointing at the talismans, "and we wanted people to see them."

The girl turned in their direction and looked at them for a moment. "They're intriguing," she said.

Bob could see Pete regain his footing. "They're Chinese talismans," Pete said, pointing again. "That one keeps away evil spirits, like demons."

"Does it work?" the girl asked, smiling for the first time.

"Do you see any demons?" Pete said.

"You're right," she said. "I don't. But I've got a cousin who's a demon. Maybe it could keep him away from me."

She stood under the Talisman Against Demons, studying it intently for what seemed to Bob a very long time. To Pete, her stillness and silence were excruciating.

Finally, he said, "Are you new in town or something? I don't think we've ever met before."

The girl gave Pete a considering look, then went back to studying the talisman.

At last she answered. "My father was Scottish, but my mother was born in Rocky Beach, and her brother still lives here. My parents met when my dad was on a consulting job, and although I was born in California, I've lived in Scotland all my life. After Dad died, my mother decided to bring me back here. We've only been here a couple of weeks."

"Gosh, I'm sorry about your dad," Pete said.

The girl shrugged. "Thanks," she said. "But I don't like to talk about it."

"So you live here now? In Rocky Beach?" Pete asked.

"Not exactly," the girl said. "My

mother's promised to take me back to Scotland in two years if I still don't like it here by then. In the meantime, she seems to think I need to be friends with my dreadful cousins. I've been bicycling around for hours, just to get away from them – particularly the older one bragging about his sports car. I wouldn't have stopped, but from a distance I thought that suit of armor might be real."

Pete said, "You like armor?"

"And swords, and crossbows, and battle-axes and halberds, and dirks and daggers and cutlasses," the girl said.

"Yikes!" said Pete. "You like *weapons*?"

"Why not? I like all kinds of stuff, and weapons are a concrete chronicle of history," the girl said.

"Jeez! You sounded like Jupiter when you said that."

The girl glanced in Bob's direction.

"Is that Jupiter? Why does he look like he's waiting for a taxi?"

"That's Bob – Bob Andrews. Jupiter – Jupiter Jones – is just around the corner. We *are* waiting for a taxi, sort of. I'm Pete Crenshaw, by the way. What's *your* name?"

"Mallory MacLeod," the girl said.

"Mallory MacLeod," Pete repeated.

"Well, that certainly *sounds* Scottish," he added. "Speaking of Scotland, have you ever heard of John Muir?"

"Of course," Mallory said. "We have a John Muir Day in Scotland. There's a hiking trail called the John Muir Way. It's a hundred thirty miles long, and I hiked most of it a couple of years ago."

Then, as Bob listened, he heard Pete repeat, almost verbatim, everything he himself had told Pete the day before about John Muir.

Bob was startled at how much Pete had retained of their conversation — though *not* startled that Pete was once again trying to impress a girl he didn't know. Pete had been doing that for years now — and ever since he and Pete and Jupiter had formed The Three Investigators, he'd added a new wrinkle to his meet-and-greet technique.

Now, he often managed to hand the girl a Three Investigators card — sometimes even implying that he and Jupiter and Bob might need the help of what Pete insisted on calling a "girl operative," if the right case came along.

"And," added Pete, still talking. "Did you know that the Scots were actually the first Europeans who made it to North America? They crossed the Atlantic with the Vikings. I read a book about it in the Rocky Beach library."

Actually, Bob had been the one who'd read the book, and Mallory somehow seemed to guess that – or so it seemed to Bob – just as a vintage Rolls-Royce with large protruding headlights pulled slowly up outside the iron gates and came to a stop.

"Here's our taxi," Pete said. "What do you think?"

Mallory stared at the car, gleaming in the sunlight.

"Cars are one kind of stuff I don't really care that much about," she said.

"Well, I don't, either," Pete said, lying. "But Bob and Jupe and I are The Three Investigators, and we need one for our work."

As Bob watched, he saw Pete reach into his pocket and hand her one of the newly printed Three Investigators cards.

"At the bottom is the office phone at Headquarters," he pointed out. "In case you need us for some reason."

Mallory looked from the Rolls to the card and back again with a combination of skepticism and interest. She put the card in her pocket, walked over to her bike, mounted, and started to pedal. As she rode away from the

Salvage Yard, she waved goodbye to Pete, and after Pete waved back, he yelled, "Jupe! The Rolls is here!" as Worthington emerged from the driver's door.

Ten minutes later, Pete and his two friends were headed out of Rocky Beach and down the Pacific Coast Highway in the Rolls, the three boys settled in the back. Although Worthington had long since stopped wearing a formal chauffeur's outfit, he was snappily dressed and wearing a blue blazer. Jupiter sat behind him, with Bob in the middle and Pete to his right – all of them watching the Pacific sparkle in the afternoon sun.

Pete wiggled his shoulders, sinking into the soft leather of the car's plush upholstery. Pete loved all cars – he'd only been trying to be agreeable when he told Mallory he didn't – but the Rolls was in a class by itself. It was like something out of a James Bond movie. It had a mini-refrigerator stocked with soda, an old-fashioned car phone they no longer needed, and enough leg room so that Pete could stretch his legs all the way out.

On the whole, he was happy with the way his talk with Mallory MacLeod had gone –

though she had certainly kept him on his toes.

The fact was, Pete liked girls a lot more than either of his friends did – or so it seemed to him. But then he'd always been the most outgoing of the three, and for years he'd been suggesting that they consider finding a girl to join the firm. He knew this annoyed Jupe, but he really couldn't help it.

Still, he did see Jupe's point. After all, they were The Three Investigators, not The Four Detectives.

Bob sat writing in his notebook and Jupiter was lost in his own thoughts, but Pete felt like talking and cleared his throat.

"I met the coolest girl," he began.

"I noticed," Bob said, smiling.

"I was telling Jupiter," Pete said, a little defensively. "Anyway, Jupe, she's from Scotland and she likes weapons and armor, but she doesn't seem to like Rocky Beach. At least not yet. I think I made a good impression."

"To tell you the truth," Bob said, "she didn't look all that impressed."

Pete was stung. "What do you mean?"

"She was sort of cool. Unenthusiastic. Pete gave her one of our cards," Bob told Jupiter. "In case she wanted to call him."

"I did not!" Pete said. "I mean, I gave

her a card, but not so she could call me."

"No," Bob said. "Of course not. Just in case she loses her bicycle and wants us to help her track it down."

"Jeez!" Pete said. "I was just being friendly. Besides, I felt sorry for her, having lost her father and everything, and then having to leave the country she'd lived in all her life."

At this, Jupiter looked up and said, "By 'lost her father,' I assume you mean her father recently died?"

"Yes," said Pete, and only then did he realize that Jupiter and Mallory were the only kids he'd ever met who had no living fathers. That would be tough, Pete thought.

And then he remembered that while Bob was upset because Mr. Sebastian was moving to Wyoming, Jupiter was probably even more upset because they'd also be saying goodbye to Worthington soon. Pete and Bob would miss him, too, but not as much as Jupe would.

Pete leaned forward and raised his voice. "We didn't tell you yet, Worthington," he said, "but we just learned Mr. Sebastian is moving to Wyoming."

"I've never been to Wyoming," Worthington said.

"Me neither!" Pete said emphatically.

"Anyway, Mr. Sebastian said he's going there to write a different kind of mystery novel – one set in the Old West."

"I was once in a movie set in the Old West," said Worthington. "I played a British detective who'd been hired by the Pinkerton Agency. I enjoyed that role quite a bit."

"I bet you did!" Pete said. "I'm always trying to get my dad to get me a part in a Western. Or at least to invite me onto a Western set. If you don't mind me asking, did you ever think about stopping driving the Rolls and trying to get back into movies?"

Worthington looked in the rear view mirror and smiled.

"To tell you the truth, Pete, I recently learned that the Rent-'n'-Ride is going to retire the Rolls in the not-too-distant future," Worthington said. "It's too expensive to maintain and more of a conversation piece than a useful means of transportation.

"I may work for the company for another month or two," he added, "but after that, I'm going to be setting off on my own. Between my work as a chauffeur and the residuals from my film roles, I've managed to put a good bit of money away, and I have only myself to look after. I don't want to go back to acting, but I *am* ready for something new. Being my own boss will be a nice change at my stage of life.”

“Maybe you could specialize in driving for detectives!” Pete said.

“Or mystery writers,” said Bob.

“Even before I met The Three Investigators, I was interested in what might be called the fundamental mysteries of life,” said Worthington. “Particularly the mystery of how human character and human intelligence interact. The movies used to explore that. Now they mostly explore how quickly and violently you can blow things up.”

Pete *liked* those kinds of movies – at least sometimes – but he wasn’t surprised to hear Jupiter say, “The study of character is the linchpin of all good detective work.”

“The psychology of the individual,” Worthington agreed.

“Also,” Jupiter said, “I’ve noticed that in the real world, no one is totally good or totally bad. People are born with definite strengths and weaknesses, and one of the tragedies of human life is that many peoples’ weaknesses are indulged by others.”

“Turning them into what are commonly known, in American movies, as bad guys. Of course, bad guys rarely think of themselves as being that," Worthington said.

This was why Jupe would miss Worthington so much, Pete thought. They often had conversations like this – conversations Pete had a hard time taking part in. Out the window a pair of seagulls floated on the wind. Below, the surf crashed silently against the rocky cliffs.

Impulsively, Pete said, "Would you like to come camping with us while we've still got the Rolls? We've been thinking of maybe taking a trip up to the Gold Country or Yosemite or somewhere. We don't have a lot of money left in the piggy bank, but I'm sure we could stretch it to pay for food for all of us."

"What a great idea, Pete," Jupiter said. "We would consider it an honor, Worthington. But, of course, the Rent-'n'-Ride would have to agree to let you go for five or six days all at once."

"I think I might be able to persuade them," said Worthington, smiling. "We couldn't take the Rolls, of course, but I'm sure they'd be happy to let me drive another vehicle – perhaps a four-wheel drive of some kind. I have quite a lot of experience driving in rough terrain, and I've been to the Gold Country before. But surely you'll be working on your new case in the coming days?"

"That's right," said Pete. Why hadn't he thought of that? Maybe because so far, the "case," such as it was, sounded as if it would just be research. He wasn't that great at research and liked cases where there was a lot of running around. He shone at running around, he thought.

The Rolls slowed down as Worthington reached the turn to Hector Sebastian's house. The mountains south of Rocky Beach were cut by deep canyons whose steep hillsides and rocky outcrops had not deterred developers.

An old estate that had featured in the boys' discovery of the jewel known as the Fiery Eye — up at the head of the canyon — had been bought and broken up into parcels. The once-secluded hills were now dotted with expensive homes and mansions, and Hector Sebastian's was about three miles up Dial Canyon Road — perched high enough so that you could see the Pacific from the outdoor patio.

Pete sat forward and watched in anticipation as Worthington drove up the gravel drive.

Hector Sebastian's house was mock-Tudor, its white stucco façade crossed by dark wood beams. Out back was a patio with a red and white striped awning, a swimming pool, and a small guest house. The swimming pool was surrounded by a fence.

Worthington stopped before the cement walkway that led to the door and the boys got out. "I'll be right over there," Worthington said, pointing to the shade thrown by the detached garage and workshop.

As Worthington pulled the car away, Pete felt the thrill he always felt at the beginning of a new case. Who knew where it would take him, and what he'd be called on to do? He hoped, as always, that he'd be up to the challenge.

Jupiter turned to him and Bob. He seemed a bit stirred up as he said, in a careful tone, "That was a fine idea of yours, Pete, about Worthington coming camping with us. Even if we need to put it off for a while, it will be something to look forward to after we conclude our current case. But for now, we need to concentrate on the task at hand.

"And since this may be the last case we ever get from Mr. Sebastian," he added, "let's be sure we do our very best."

Pete's heart began to pound as Jupiter knocked three times – once for each of The

Three Investigators – on the wooden door with the metal strapping. Their first case of the summer was about to start!

5

A New Case

Jupiter was feeling more unsettled than usual as he stood on the stoop knocking. He was surprised at how quickly his knock was answered. He'd barely lowered his arm when Hector Sebastian opened the door. The pipe the mystery writer couldn't seem to stop smoking was clenched in his right hand.

"Good afternoon, my friends," Mr. Sebastian said. "Thanks for coming. Let's get you some refreshments before I introduce you to Isabella Chang. She's waiting on the patio. I offered her lemonade and cookies, but she preferred a cup of black tea."

He led the boys through an entry hall and into a comfortable kitchen where a pitcher of lemonade was waiting on a tray. Three glasses and a plate of cookies surrounded it, and when Mr. Sebastian gestured invitingly toward Pete, he dashed over to pick the tray up. Mr. Sebastian chuckled. Jupiter knew he always offered The Three Investigators lemonade, a reference to *The Secret of Terror Castle*, in which they'd also been offered lemonade –

though in *that* case the lemonade had been a clue which helped them solve the mystery.

After that, Mr. Sebastian led them through his house – where bookcases had been built almost everywhere, and colorful flat rugs dotted the floor. Out back, on the patio, under the awning, an older woman sat upright, looking toward the sea. She had the posture of a woman of half her years, though the skin on her arms was mottled with age marks. Under her wispy eyebrows, her almond eyes were dark and bright with intelligence. Pete set the tray with the lemonade on a table.

"Boys," Mr. Sebastian said. "I'd like you to meet my good friend, Isabella Chang. Isabella, these are The Three Investigators – Bob Andrews, Pete Crenshaw, and Jupiter Jones."

Each of the boys went over to shake her hand politely when his name was mentioned. When Jupiter got there, he said, "We're very pleased to meet you, Ms. Chang," then handed her The Three Investigators' business card.

Her hand was cool as she took it. She studied it carefully and then looked up.

"Please sit down," she said. "And please proceed with Hector's refreshments."

Pete went to the table which held the lemonade tray, then poured three glasses –

handing two to his friends – and grabbed a handful of cookies. They all took seats, and Hector Sebastian sat in a chair beside Isabella Chang. She finished studying the card, then said, "These question marks. What do they mean?"

Jupiter smiled. It never failed. "The question mark is the universal symbol of something unknown," he said. "Our firm stands ready to investigate anything – any puzzle or riddle, mystery or conundrum brought to our attention. The three questions marks are our trademark, and together they always stand for The Three Investigators."

"Very impressive," Ms. Chang said. "I was also impressed when Hector outlined the history of your firm. Impressed by you, but also by your parents – for giving you the same freedoms *they* had when they were growing up."

"They give us a lot of freedom to go where we want and investigate when we get there," Bob said, "but they've all put their feet down about technology – especially smart phones and tablets. My mom says our brains are still developing and too much technology can hurt them."

"Very wise of her," said Ms. Chang. "There's a difference between wisdom and knowledge. A big one. How did the three of you come to form an investigative firm? And why is Jupiter the First Investigator?"

"Because he's a gen – Because he's so smart!" exclaimed Pete. When he heard what Pete was about to say, Jupiter winced and was grateful when Pete didn't say it after all.

Bob took over the explanation. "It's not just that. Jupiter is a born leader. Even in kindergarten, on the playground, he was always taking charge. He'd get frustrated with any kids who just sat around, waiting for something to happen."

"Pete and Bob are just as smart as I am – though in a different way," Jupiter said firmly. "And without Pete's courage and kindness and Bob's diligence and attention to detail, The Three Investigators would never have been successful."

"There's nothing better than the esteem of those who know you well," said Isabella Chang. "So, let's get down to why we're all here today. Hector has already told you about my book, I think. I need some help with research. My eyesight is getting so poor I can't read for very long, and looking at a computer screen is impossible.

"I had a friend who lived with me for a

number of years after she retired, who kept me company and helped with things my eyesight made difficult," she added. "After she died, I hired a lovely woman to help me, but she knows nothing about computers. I'm quite helpless." She smiled in a way that made Jupiter think she was anything but.

"Nonsense," said Hector Sebastian. "She's a tiger. Don't let her fool you." Jupiter thought Mr. Sebastian had it about right.

Isabella Chang looked at Hector with some amusement. "I'm told that more and more historical and genealogical records are showing up online every day, and I'm interested in my several-times great grandfather, a man named Li Chang. He was born in this country, but his father came from China and his mother from Ireland during the Gold Rush. Sometime between 1849 and 1853.

"As I'm sure you know, once the Gold Rush started, people from all over the world got gold fever. Almost 300,000 people came to California, and maybe 25,000 young Chinese men were among them. At first, there were no Chinese women, so when Li's father wanted to get married, he married an Irish woman instead of someone from his own country. What's of special interest to me is that Li was educated – very well-educated from what I can gather – in a one-room schoolhouse up north. My book is really about schoolhouses like that – Abecedarian Academies – but I'd like to weave Li Chang into it, if I can."

"I think there are now entire websites that can help you discover members of your family and facts about their history," Bob said. "By the way, 'abecedarian' is a cool word."

"Yes," said Isabella Chang. "I can't remember where I first encountered it, but I've always loved it. It comes from the Latin *abecedarius*, which means *alphabetical*, and it entered English usage in the 17th century. Back then it meant someone engaged in teaching the alphabet, but now it refers more to the students who are learning it.

"In the nineteenth and early twentieth centuries, one-room schools were everywhere," she continued. "They were, for the most part, simple wood-frame buildings – heated, if at all, by a wood stove. Outside there were separate outhouses for the boys and girls. Teachers could have as few as six or seven students or as many as eighteen or nineteen – often from only a handful of families. The schools ran from first grade through eighth grade. After eighth grade, you were finished with your education and ready to make a life for yourself."

Jupiter blinked in surprise. He and his friends had just graduated from eighth grade, and although he had certainly started thinking about what he might want to do when he grew up – just now, he was wondering whether he might become an inventor – he was glad he wouldn't need to decide for a while yet.

"My research suggests," said Isabella Chang, "that contrary to what you might think, the children in these schools – the abecedarians – received an education both rigorous and complete. Li Chang was a student at a tiny schoolhouse in a hamlet near the town of Cool.

"His teacher was a cousin of his mother's who had come with her from Ireland – a man who had grown up at a time when Catholics had no schools of their own. He himself had learned in one of the illegal secret schools – called "hedge schools" – where Catholic children were taught. He came to America not in search of treasure but to give it away to others," she explained.

"Wow," Pete said. "Did they really have schools in hedges?"

Isabella Chang laughed. "Maybe," she said. "But also in houses, sheds, and barns – anywhere the authorities weren't looking. According to the stories passed down in my family, this man, whose name I don't know, was quite remarkable and extraordinarily well-educated – he knew Greek and Latin, mathematics and botany. He came to America to teach, and so he became the schoolmaster at the Abecedarian Academy near Cool."

"What else do you know about Li Chang?" Jupiter asked.

"Not very much," Isabella Chang admitted, "which is why I want your help. But there is one more thing. I don't know if Hector mentioned anything to you about this or not, but Li Chang's father was murdered. There's a rumor in my family that he'd had real success panning for gold and was killed for his treasure. But there's nothing at all to substantiate that, and I'm afraid the truth is probably more depressing – that he was murdered because he was Chinese. Growing up, I was told that after Li's father was killed, he and his mother moved to the town of Auburn and started a laundry there."

She sat and thought for a minute. "I know there's something else I wanted to tell you. Oh, yes, the only other thing I know about Li Chang is that he was associated with the Auburn Public Library. Of course, I don't *really* know that, but it was part of my family's oral tradition. The library was opened in 1910 or thereabouts and was one of many libraries in California built with help from a grant from Andrew Carnegie."

"I know about Carnegie Libraries," Bob said. "The Rocky Beach public library isn't one, but I did a school project on them once. Andrew Carnegie supplied the money to help build a total of 2,500 of them, across the whole of the United States. When he was a boy living in the East, and working for the local telegraph company, Carnegie was able to borrow books from the personal library of his employer."

"Yes," said Isabella Chang. "In those days, a lot of people thought that 'working boys' (as they called them then) shouldn't be allowed to read books, so Carnegie was very grateful to his mentor, and never forgot the debt he owed to those who helped him. He was a great philanthropist who gave away 90 percent of his fortune in the last years of his life. He said he thought that people ought to spend the first third of their lives getting as much education as they could, the second third making as much money as they could, and the last third giving it all away to worthwhile causes."

Although Jupiter knew almost nothing

about Andrew Carnegie, he was impressed by the elegance of this idea. He also found himself liking Isabella Chang. He had always liked adults who assumed that young people should be treated as intellectual equals.

"I don't think the original Carnegie library in Auburn is a library any more," Isabella Chang added, "but I know it's still standing. I've been told it's an arts center now. You boys probably have no idea how radical an idea free libraries were – just a little over a hundred years ago. Free libraries, free education – both leading to free thought."

At this, Pete, who had been sitting trying to contain himself, suddenly burst out.

"But maybe Li's father *did* find gold. Why not? A lot of people must have, if they came from all over the world to find it. And maybe he managed to hide his treasure from whoever killed him."

Both Bob and Hector Sebastian laughed.

"That might happen in a book like *Treasure Island*, Pete, but in real life, if he *was* killed for his gold, that gold ended up in someone else's pocket," Hector said.

"I'm sorry," said Isabella Chang. "I'm afraid the only gold you're going to discover on this case is the kind you can stock your minds with. I envy you boys your adventure," she added. "I spent my life teaching history and know that finding out about the past can change the way you think about the future. You boys are in high school now?"

"We start in the fall," Jupiter said.

"That's exciting," Isabella Chang said. "I'm sure you'll all do very well."

At that, Hector Sebastian stood up and took an envelope from the inside pocket of his sports coat. "I told you I had two things to give you. The first is obviously this case. Here's the other. It's a going-away present of sorts — though I'm the one who's going away."

He handed the envelope to Jupiter who opened it and stared in amazement at a small packet of dollars. There seemed to be mostly tens and twenties, but there were also three or four hundred dollar bills.

"Golly," Jupiter said. "I don't know what to say, Mr. Sebastian."

"Don't say anything," Hector Sebastian said. "It's seed money, really. Sure, you can do research in the library and on the Internet, but you've always excelled at hands-on sleuthing, and I think you boys need to get up to the Gold Country to see the places where Li Chang and his family lived. Maybe his one-room school-house is still standing. And although there are fires burning in northern California, the fires are to the north and west of both Auburn and Cool, and the smoke is blowing in the opposite direction."

"That's a great idea, Mr. Sebastian," Jupiter said. "We've got some time left on the Rolls, and maybe Worthington can drive us."

"There's nothing like on-the-ground investigating for gumshoes like the three of you," Hector Sebastian said.

"I promise we'll use your money well," Jupiter said.

"I know you will, Jupiter," said Hector Sebastian. "Is there anything else you want to say, Isabella?"

Isabella Chang sat forward in her chair and nodded.

"Now that I'm sure you'll be going to the Gold Country, I should tell you that I have a somewhat distant cousin who lives up in Auburn. John Chang is a real estate developer, but he's also the head of the Gold Country Historical Society. I'll call him to let him know you're coming. You should write his name and address down," she said.

"We will, Ms. Chang," Jupiter said.

"We'll be in touch. Do you use e-mail?"

Isabella pointed to her eyes. "Better to call me, Jupiter," she said. She gave them her telephone number and the information about John Chang, and Bob wrote it all down carefully in his notebook. He also programmed her number into his cellphone.

Hector Sebastian walked them to the door. "We won't say goodbye," he told the boys. "I've only rented the house outside of Dubois for a year, and although I may end up staying longer, I'm not going to sell this house. I'm going to rent it out to another writer. And you can always call or e-mail me in Wyoming. In fact, maybe you and I can Skype or Zoom sometime," he said to Bob.

"That would be great," Bob said. "I've never done it, but I bet it's fun."

"It can be," said Hector Sebastian. "And although I'm sure you'll do a splendid job writing up the cases of The Three Investigators without any help from me, please feel free to get in touch any time at all."

Jupiter watched Bob's face light up in the biggest smile he'd seen since they'd received news that Hector Sebastian was leaving California. Jupiter shook Mr. Sebastian's hand, then led the way back to Worthington and the

Rolls. His unsettled feeling had gone away while he listened to Isabella Chang talk about education and libraries and free thought – with a little talk about gold and murder thrown in.

In fact, he had the growing feeling that the Isabella Chang case was going to turn into something more complex and puzzling than he had thought it would at first. Pete and Bob clearly thought so, too, because when they had climbed back into the Rolls, and Worthington had made his way back down the driveway and out onto Dial Canyon Road, they both started talking to him excitedly about what lay ahead.

"Hector Sebastian gave us a going away present of a trip up to the Gold Country!" said Pete. "Our new case is from an old Chinese woman whose ancestor was probably murdered for his gold. It may even still be there! Will you be able to drive us? Maybe we could go to Yosemite on the same trip!"

"We're going to Auburn, mainly," said Bob, "but probably also to some place near a town called Cool – especially if the one-room schoolhouse where Li Chang was educated is still standing. I have a lot of research to do before we go, but if I'm lucky, I can get most of it done tomorrow. Would you really come camping with us? Maybe we could also rent a cabin somewhere. Where did you go when *you* were in the Gold Country?"

"I drove for a while for a man who had a mansion outside the town of Jackson," said Worthington, smiling. "The area was originally inhabited by the northern Sierra Indians, but the town of Jackson was built during the Gold Rush. As I said, I'll have to check with my boss at the Rent-'n'-Ride about the dates, but since we wouldn't be taking the Rolls, I can see no reason why not. He has an old Land Rover that hardly ever gets rented. Quite a change for all of us from the days when you were Masters' Jones, Crenshaw, and Andrews."

As Worthington spoke, he was taking the Rolls around a hairpin curve, and as the car emerged on the other side – where a very sharp incline climbed toward the eastern sky – Jupiter happened to be looking up when he saw a large rock break loose and come tumbling down the slope straight toward Dial Canyon Road.

"Look out!" he said to Worthington, but Worthington had already seen the danger. He smoothly applied the brakes and turned just far enough to the right to avoid the rock without going off the road. Worthington, Jupiter thought, was both an inspiring man and an extraordinary driver!

6

An Irish Curse

The next morning, bright and early, Bob commandeered an entire table at the Rocky Beach Library. By then, Worthington had confirmed that he and a car would be available for the coming week, and Jupe and Pete were at the Salvage Yard, checking their camping gear and packing for two nights in Yosemite.

When they'd gotten back to Rocky Beach the day before, the three of them had gone into Headquarters, booted up the firm's computer, and checked on Google Maps to see how easily they might squeeze in a stop there while they were driving up to Auburn. As it turned out, the National Park was almost on the way.

Of course, they'd had a moment of disappointment – verging, in Pete's case, on panic – when they'd discovered that campsites in Yosemite were booked as long as six months ahead. But they'd been lucky; a large group had recently canceled multiple reservations, and Bob had been able to grab one of the open campsites.

On the way from Yosemite up to Auburn, they planned to drive through Jackson, where Worthington had worked. The Roaring Camp Mining Company and the Kennedy Gold Mine were close by. They'd found a place that rented cabins not far from Auburn and had made reservations there as well.

For now, though, Bob had research to do — research about Li Chang. The afternoon before, on Hector Sebastian's patio, he'd been more excited than he'd let on when Isabella Chang mentioned the Carnegie Library in Auburn. When he'd been working on his Carnegie project, he'd discovered that the Rocky Beach Library had a lot of bound volumes of old Auburn newspapers in the storerooms in its basement.

The Auburn *Journal* had been founded in 1872, and although Bob didn't yet know the answers to some very important questions — for example, when Li Chang's mother and father had gotten married, when Li had been born, or when his father had died — since Isabella Chang had said Li's parents had come over during the height of the Gold Rush, Li couldn't have been more than twenty when the Auburn *Journal* was founded.

If he'd lived long enough to see the

Auburn Library go up, there should be almost forty years during which Li Chang might have been mentioned in the paper. With Miss Bennett's permission, Bob had hauled all the Auburn volumes up into the library, and after looking quickly through them, had logged onto his laptop.

The library had computers for the use of library patrons, but Bob was getting used to using his, and the night before he had bookmarked several genealogical websites. The one that looked most promising had an introductory offer of seven free days, so Bob had signed up for it. At first, he was afraid that since "Chang" was such a common Chinese name, it might be difficult for him to find out anything solid about Isabella Chang's ancestor, but he hit the jackpot when he discovered a family tree whose creator and owner permitted anyone to view it.

The owner's name wasn't Chang, but he was related to Li Chang somehow, and the family tree had Li's date and place of birth and death, the full names of both his parents, and their dates and places of birth and death. It also had the name and date of birth and death of Li's father's much younger brother, Hao Chang.

From the dates, Bob could see that Hao Chang had not come to California during the gold rush but almost twenty years later — in 1869 or 1870 — and Bob inferred that Hao had never even met his older brother before he arrived in America. In 1875, he had married a Chinese woman and had a number of children, so Bob deduced that, by the time he arrived, Chinese women must have been arriving, too.

However, Hao Chang was not Bob's concern, and he went back to Li Chang's entry — which also had the name of his son and his son's son, and so on, down to Isabella Chang — and links to several recent articles in the Auburn *Journal* in which his name was mentioned. Li Chang has been born in 1859 and had died during the great flu epidemic of 1918 — at the age of 59. The genealogy website also had a photograph of Li Chang's gravestone.

The gravestone seemed to be of marble, and a hundred years of rainy seasons had blurred the words which had been carved into it. Still, in addition to Li Chang's dates of birth and death, the gravestone bore the words FREE TO ALL across the top, and had a tiny, blurry carving of something riding on the top of the "Li" section of his name.

Bob printed the photograph to show to

Pete and Jupiter later. He also printed off or wrote down all the vital information he'd found on the ancestry website. After that, he followed the links and discovered that one of the articles was about Isabella Chang's distant cousin John Chang receiving a Citizen of the Year Award for his work in the Gold Country Historical Society.

After finding out everything he could online, Bob dived into the bound volumes of the Auburn *Journal*. They smelled musty and pulpy, and the paper was quite fragile, but since it had spent a lot of the last five decades in the dark, it was in better shape than Bob would have expected. Since he now knew the Auburn Library had been dedicated in 1909, he was quickly able to find an article that mentioned that Li Chang had been asked to choose books for a special Chinese section of the library – to serve the residents of what was then the Auburn version of Chinatown.

Bob also found an article about the laundry which Li and his mother – and when she died, Li and his wife – had owned and operated. It had been a multipurpose business, with a dry goods section, and a corner where customers could sit in comfortable chairs and read books from a built-in floor-to-ceiling bookcase while they waited to pick up laundry – and where Li and his wife also served them tea. Moving back in time to 1873 – the year of Li's father's death – Bob was once again lucky and found an article about his murder right away.

That article contained the first big surprise Bob encountered in his research, because it stated that Li Chang's father had been shot to death by another Chinese man – and therefore *not*, as Isabella Chang had suggested, because he was Chinese. According to the Auburn *Journal*, Li's father's Irish widow, Rose O'Malley Chang, had actually seen her husband shot, but when asked for descriptions of his attacker, had said she could see nothing clearly but that he was Chinese.

As an experienced investigator who had, on occasion, worn disguises himself, Bob found this detail suspicious. After all, in the first decades after Chinese men had arrived in California, they had braided their waist-length black hair in traditional Chinese pigtails. The pigtails would have been easy to fake, Bob thought, if you had wanted to look Chinese from a distance.

Rose Chang was also reported to have insisted that the treasure in gold that her husband was rumored to have found didn't exist, but if it *had*, she would curse it and curse it and curse it so that it wouldn't be cleansed of the curse for fifty years. In the meantime, if anyone tried to use the gold, they, too, would be cursed. Fifty years would have taken the curse to 1923, Bob thought. He smiled to himself as he imagined reassuring Pete that if there *was* lost gold, it could pose no danger now.

Bob took the bound volume to the library's copying machine. He'd just finished the laborious copying of all the relevant articles he'd found when he noticed a girl about his age talking to Miss Bennett at the Circulation Desk. From the back, especially with her shoulder-length red hair, she looked a lot like the girl Pete had been talking to the day before in the Salvage Yard. Beside her was a pile of books, and she was trying to check them out.

From a distance, Bob heard Miss Bennett saying, "Yes, of course, anyone who lives in Rocky Beach can have a library card. I just need a piece of I.D. in order to give you one."

"But I've only just moved here from Scotland," the girl replied – proving that this was indeed Mallory MacLeod. "All I've got is my Young Scot card. My mother and I are living in a boarding house called the Wessex House until our house in Scotland sells."

"I know where the Wessex House is," Miss Bennett said. "Do you have any relatives in town I might know?"

"Sylvester Norris is my mother's brother," Mallory said – though sounding as if she'd rather not admit it.

Miss Bennett said, "You mean you're Skinny Norris's *cousin?*"

"Unfortunately, yes," Mallory said.

Bob was so surprised he set the bound volumes he was holding down on the table a lot more loudly than he meant to.

Mallory turned at the sound. When she saw Bob, she looked relieved.

"He knows me," she said to Miss Bennett. "We met yesterday. Or at least I met his friend Pete."

Before he could stop himself, Bob repeated what Miss Bennett had already said. "You're Skinny Norris's *cousin?*"

The moment he said it, he felt like kicking himself, not only because of the rudeness and repetition but because he realized that if he'd been Jupiter, he'd have figured this out the day before when Pete and Mallory had been talking.

After all, when Skinny had accosted Bob the morning Miss Bennett had left him in charge of the circulation desk, Skinny had said he was supposed to be helping his aunt and her daughter – who had just moved back to Rocky Beach. He'd also said his "little cousin Mally-Wally" wasn't happy to be here at all. On top of that, when Mallory had been talking to Pete, she'd mentioned her older cousin bragging about his sports car. Three clues should have been more than enough, Bob thought.

It had really been very slow of him not to put the first clue and the second one together – though really, who on earth *would* imagine that Mallory and Skinny were cousins? They seemed to Bob as different as human beings could be.

A few minutes later, Bob had convinced Miss Bennett to issue Mallory a library card, and while the librarian was scanning the bar codes, he snuck a look at the titles. Most of them seemed to be fantasies, but one of them was a Robert Heinlein science fiction novel and one was *Gulliver's Travels*. He'd never read it, but he knew that, although it was fantastical, it was actually a satire from the 18th century.

The whole time, Bob tried to come up with something clever to say but couldn't, and when Mallory started to stuff her library books into her backpack, he found himself apologizing.

"Sorry about what I said before," he told her. "It's just that Skinny isn't exactly my favorite person. Also, he's got white-blond hair, and your hair is really red."

"I wish I *didn't* have red hair," Mallory said. "It makes me feel like some kind of Celtic cliché."

Miss Bennett cleared her throat. "If you two want to talk," she said kindly, "please take your conversation outside. Bob, you can come back to return the journals to the basement."

Hurriedly, Bob stuffed all his research and his laptop into his backpack while Mallory waited. Today she was wearing blue jeans and a black t-shirt, and Bob couldn't help but notice how strikingly this clothing set off the red of her hair and the steely blue of her eyes. He followed her out of the library, and by the time they'd reached the bike rack on the sidewalk, he'd gotten up the courage to talk to her properly.

"Why did you say that about your hair?" he said. "Do you have a fiery temper?"

"I get impatient pretty fast, but I don't get really angry unless someone is being a complete and total muppet or a git."

Bob's confusion must have shown on his

face, because she said, rather kindly, "Gits are jerks and muppets are idiots. They're UK slang – but what I actually meant about my hair being red was just that I'd rather not stick out in a crowd."

Good luck with that, Bob thought, but what he said was, "I know what you mean. I don't like to stick out, either. In fact, one reason I like reading novels is that, in novels, only muppets and gits stick out much."

"Exactly," Mallory said. "And when you read a novel, you can become someone else entirely – someone from a different sex or race or even *species* from the one you were born as."

When Mallory said this, Bob looked at her with real respect. Unlike a lot of the kids he met these days, this was a interesting girl with an interesting mind. He liked her. In fact, he was starting to like her a lot.

"What did your father do in Scotland?" Bob asked. "I heard you telling Pete about him. My friend Jupiter also lost his father when he was young. It's his uncle who owns the Salvage Yard, but Jupiter's nothing at all like his Uncle Titus."

"My father was an engineer," Mallory said. "He built bridges. Before my mother met him, she was a costume designer for the movies, and she thought it would be easier for her to get full-time work if she moved back to Hollywood after he died. But she promised me we'd go back to Scotland in two years if I couldn't get used to living here."

"Pete's father works in the movies, too," Bob said. "He's a construction manager on film sets. Pete and Jupiter and I are very different, but we've been best friends since kindergarten, and we work really well together."

"Don't worry," Mallory said. "I liked Pete. He was trying hard with all that stuff about John Muir and the Vikings. Also, when he said, 'Do you see any demons?' I had to stop myself from laughing. I hadn't expected him to make a joke like that. He seems to really like people, and he was fun to be around."

Bob was so impressed by this analysis of Pete that for a moment he didn't know what to say, but finally he responded. "He's also as brave as a lion in a pinch. A little superstitious, but really, really brave."

"I'm sure he is," Mallory said. "So what's the head of The Three Investigators like? I looked at the card Pete gave me. I even looked the three of you up online."

Though Bob was stunned by this information, he tried to keep it to himself.

"Jupiter?" Bob asked. "He knows almost everything. He's a long-term planner and very, very focused. He's good at explaining complicated stuff in a simple way, but he's also good at building things. He's the one who thought of hanging the Chinese talismans across the front of the Salvage Yard's office."

Though Bob thought this was a very inadequate description of Jupiter's talents, Mallory nodded as if she understood.

"I wonder who drew those talismans in the first place," she said. "I don't know anything about Chinese culture – just a bit about its weaponry, but not much even about that."

"I really don't know much about it either," Bob said. "My mom's Chinese, but my dad is Scottish/Norse. In fact, you and I might even be related. Not cousins, like you and Skinny, but related somehow." He paused. "I've never met a girl who was interested in weaponry before."

"It's not just weapons," Mallory said. "I like *things*. Material culture of all kinds. I remember the details about objects. Also, I have a sort of natural instinct that lets me sort real things out from imitations."

Bob laughed. "Jupiter's Aunt Mathilda has that instinct, too. In *her* case, it's about making money. She'd rather put me and Pete and Jupiter to work than let us do investigations."

"What case are you working on now?" Mallory asked.

"We're finding out about the ancestor of a woman who's writing a book about one-room schoolhouses in California. A man who lived up in the Gold Country. There are rumors that his father was killed for a bag of gold, and Pete wants to believe the gold is still there somewhere. But the guy actually owned a laundry in the town of Auburn. We're going to be driving up there in a few days. On the way, we're stopping in Yosemite to go camping."

"That's sounds great," Mallory said. "I'd love to do some real camping myself, but my mother is taking me to a Scottish music camp up near Grass Valley for a week, to try to make me happier about moving to California. I don't like fiddle music much, and a week of it is going to drive me crazy, but she was so excited about her idea I couldn't bear to tell her no."

"I think Grass Valley's not that far from Auburn," Bob said. "There's a library in Auburn that was funded by Andrew Carnegie."

"Really?" Mallory said. "I didn't know

he built libraries in America, but I've been to the one in Dunfermline, where he was born. I grew up not far from there."

She paused and looked at Bob. "Well, I guess I better get going," she said. "My mother wants us to get packed."

"If you'll really be in Grass Valley when the three of us are in Auburn, maybe we'll run into you," Bob said.

"That'd be a lot more fun than music camp," Mallory said. "But I'm not sure I'll be able to get away."

Bob paused, then risked it. "I'm not really supposed to use my cellphone just to talk to other kids, but as Records and Research for The Three Investigators, I'm taking the phone with me on our trip. The number's on our card if you want to call me while we're both up north."

"Maybe I will," Mallory said.

She still didn't have a bike helmet. Impulsively, Bob asked, "Don't you wear bike helmets in Scotland? In California, everyone under seventeen is supposed to."

"You're kidding," Mallory said. "I've never worn a helmet in my life. Except when I went climbing with my father. But that was a different kind."

"You could probably use that one," Bob said. "No one's going to arrest you or anything if you don't, but I think your mother might have to pay some sort of fine if you do it too often."

"Good grief," said Mallory. "I thought America was the land of the free and the home of the brave. Well, thanks for telling me. I'll see you around."

"I hope so," Bob found himself saying.

After she rode away, Bob returned the bound volumes of newspapers to the basement, then got on his own bike and pedaled as fast as he could to the Salvage Yard. When he pushed his bike through Green Gate One, he saw that the outside workshop was filled with a big pile of camping gear and also groceries for the two nights they planned to spend in Yosemite.

Pete was sharpening his sheath knife while Jupe was cleaning and oiling his Swiss Army knife – which had everything from a tweezer to scissors, a corkscrew, an awl, and a screwdriver. By the time Bob joined them, Pete and Jupiter had already resealed the seams on the tents.

Luckily, they had *two* tents – one older and one newer – so Worthington could have his own. They also had an extra sleeping bag that Hans had given them before he married and left the Salvage Yard. Bob helped his friends pack the equipment into duffel bags, and when they were finished, they went into Headquarters to review the research Bob had done.

There was a lot to go over, already, so Bob focused on what Rose Chang had said about a Chinese man having shot her husband, and the curse she had put on any gold her husband might actually have owned. As Bob had thought he might, Pete seemed alarmed by the curse, so Bob pointed out that even if cursing really worked, in *this* case, the curse would have expired almost a hundred years before.

Bob also told his friends that, from the dates, he surmised that Li Chang must have been thirteen years old – and still in eighth grade – when his father was killed, about six months before he graduated from the one-room schoolhouse.

At first, Bob thought he wouldn't mention running into Mallory MacLeod, but since he'd told her to call him if she wanted, he thought he'd better. He reminded Jupiter about Pete meeting her in the Salvage Yard and giving her a card, then told them both what had happened at the library.

"Her father was an engineer and her mother is looking for work as a costume designer," Bob said. "But the most amazing thing is that she's Skinny Norris's cousin."

Pete let out a yelp of astonishment.

"What's amazing about that?" Jupiter asked.

"Well, she's nothing like him," Bob said. "She's smart and nice and interesting. And you know what Skinny is like."

Jupiter said, ""Even within a nuclear family, there are often big genetic variations. Intelligence and many other traits are highly heritable, but Skinny and his cousin only share a single set of grandparents, so 50% of their genetic material comes from the other set of grandparents. Also, people are affected by their environments.

"To put it another way, no matter how much you know about a person's background – his parents or grandparents or great-grandparents – there's a limit to what that can tell you about the person himself, or who he might become."

Pete still seemed almost dumbstruck about Mallory and Skinny, but eventually he said, "I don't know, Jupe. Those two being cousins is the biggest example of genetic variation you're ever going to run into. It's not just that she isn't a jerk like Skinny. She said that weapons are a concrete chronicle of history, and she uses words like 'intriguing.' I think you'd actually *like* her."

"I have no reason not to," Jupiter said. "But I doubt we have very much in common."

"I wouldn't be so sure of that," said Bob. "I think you might have a lot more in common than you think."

"Only time will tell," Jupiter said.

The landline in Headquarters suddenly rang and startled all of them. While Bob cleared some of his papers out of the way, Jupiter put the phone on speaker and answered it.

"Three Investigators Headquarters," he said. "Jupiter Jones speaking."

"Jupiter, this is Isabella Chang. I'm calling to tell you something I forgot to mention when we were together at Hector Sebastian's house. I also wanted you to know that I just got off the phone with my Auburn cousin, and he plans to call you himself sometime tomorrow. I gave him both of the numbers on your card – the landline number and the cellphone. I hope that won't be inconvenient."

Actually, it *would* be inconvenient, Bob thought ruefully. Tomorrow they'd be heading for Yosemite, and the only phone they'd have with them would be his. With any luck, Chang would call in the morning – or at least before they arrived at their campsite. Bob had read that the reception was pretty poor in the park – that though you *could* get calls, the service was erratic.

Meanwhile, Jupiter was saying, "No, of course not. We'll be happy to hear from him. Although we'll be on the road by mid-morning."

"Well, you have his contact information if you need it. Anyway, the thing I forgot to tell you was that Li Chang's Irish schoolmaster apparently had a tradition of giving his best graduating student the opportunity to write a poem and inscribe it on a wooden plaque. Those plaques were hung on the walls of the schoolhouse, and when the Gold Country Museum was established in Auburn, they were collected and donated to the museum. Li Chang's was one of them, and if you go to see the collection, I'd appreciate it if you'd take a photograph of his inscription and give it to me when you get back."

"We don't have a separate camera, but Bob can take a picture with his cellphone," Jupiter assured her.

"That will be perfect," Isabella Chang said. "Goodbye, then."

"Goodbye," Jupiter said, punching off.

Bob wished he had warned Isabella Chang about the cellphone reception in Yosemite and started to say so. But Jupiter just pinched his lower lip and for the next few minutes had nothing to say to anyone as he stared thoughtfully off into space. He was clearly thinking hard.

7

A Suspicious Phone Call

The next morning Pete and Bob were scheduled to show up at the Salvage Yard at 9:00. Pete got there fifteen minutes early, and when Bob didn't arrive until just before 9:00, he'd started to get a little jumpy. Luckily, there was no reason to do so – Jupiter was on time, and the three of them had only a minute to talk to one another before Worthington pulled in driving a dark blue Land Rover.

As Worthington opened the driver's door and sprang out, Pete saw he was wearing a light plaid shirt, blue jeans, and a pair of well-worn hiking boots – evidence that he'd done a lot more in California than drive people around in a Rolls-Royce.

"Well, boys," he said, "Are you ready for our big adventure?"

"We sure are," Pete said. He eyed the front seat, next to Worthington, but thought that Jupiter probably deserved the honor. Jupiter, however, didn't think so.

"Do you want to ride shotgun, Pete?" he asked.

"Boy!" Pete said. "Do I! Thanks, Jupe. By the way, where did such a weird expression come from? I bet you know."

"As a matter of fact I do," Jupiter said. "Men who guarded strongboxes on stagecoaches rode in front of the coach, next to the driver. They carried short-barreled shotguns. Thus the term."

Although Pete was frequently astonished by how much Jupiter knew, he was also amazed at how little credit Jupiter wanted for knowing it. He seemed to like knowledge for its own sake, and though Pete did too, in a way, the truth was he really didn't. What he really liked was people, and interesting situations like this one. He was psyched to be going on a six-day trip with Worthington − to see Worthington wearing everyday clothes, and to know that he'd be there every step of the way as they worked their new case.

"I hope you like the Land Rover," Worthington said.

"I think it's fantastic," Pete said. The boys loaded their gear, then went to say goodbye to Aunt Mathilda and Uncle Titus.

"Have fun!" said Uncle Titus.

"Don't forget to eat!" said Aunt Mathilda.

The drive to Yosemite Valley was supposed to take a bit less than six hours – which meant they'd get there mid-afternoon. They zoomed up California's central valley, through Bakersfield and Fresno, where Worthington got on Route 141 headed east up into the mountains.

Jupiter was tense with energy as he stared out the window, but Bob sat with their new **GPS** in his hand, looking at the ever-changing landscape while also consulting an actual map of California. He kept reporting on their progress and exclaiming about how exact the device was.

"We've driven 156 miles, *exactly*," he said, and then later, "We've driven 180 miles," and, later still, "We have *exactly* 100 miles still to go."

Although Pete could understand Bob's fascination with pinpointing their location at every moment, he also found himself vaguely irritated. Since he'd never been all that good with maps but had an excellent sense of direction, whenever he and Jupiter and Bob had been lost in a strange place, Pete had always managed to get them on the right track to someplace solid.

In fact, his sense of direction was so

good that he was sorry to think it might not be needed as frequently in future. Of course, the GPS – and Bob – were also reporting on the Land Rover's ever-changing elevation, and *that* was something Pete could never have done. The road began to climb as Route 141 entered the foothills of the Sierras, leaving the flat hot valley behind.

Jupiter rolled down the window and stuck his hand out.

"It's cooler outside already," he said. "Tonight in Yosemite it may even get cold."

"That's what our sleeping bags are for!" Pete said. "And we'll have a fire!"

"It's lucky the Lynx Canyon fire and the ones closer to the Sierras have been contained," Jupiter said. "Or we might not have been permitted to have a fire at our campsite."

"Let's just make sure we keep an eye out for pyromaniacs," Pete said.

Firs and pines now lined the sides of the road, and the once-straight highway began to meander. Worthington slowed to adjust to the new driving conditions and Pete watched in ad-miration as he expertly braked coming into a curve.

There were now more cars on the two-lane road. They passed through the tiny towns of Sugar Pine and Fish Camp and suddenly they were there, at the South Entrance to Yosemite National Park.

"We're here," Bob exclaimed as they entered the park. "The map, the GPS, and reality all line up!"

As they passed through the long Wawona Tunnel, Pete marveled at how men had carved their way right through the rock. On the other side, Worthington pulled over into a large parking area, and all four got out of the car.

"Holy moly!" Pete said in awe.

"I read about this," Bob said. "They call it Tunnel View. I think it's where John Muir and other Europeans saw the Yosemite Valley for the first time."

To the left, the impressive sheer face of El Capitan rose thousands of feet above the Merced River.

"There's Half Dome," Jupiter said, pointing to a mountain of rock that looked as though it had been cleaved in two. "And Bridalveil Falls."

"All I can do is wonder whether my phone is going to ring," Bob said. "I've been waiting all day and John Chang still hasn't called."

"That's right!" Pete said.

"What a way to ruin a wonderful trip," Bob added.

"You should put it out of your mind for now," said Jupiter.

Several hours later they had put up the tents, built a fire, cooked dinner, and cleaned up — and since John Chang still hadn't called, Bob decided to *really* put it out of his mind by switching off his cellphone and helping Pete and Jupiter tend the fire. They hadn't let Worthington help with anything, so he was sitting happily in a camp chair, reading about the animals of Yosemite.

"There are bobcats in the park," he said. "Also golden eagles and bighorn sheep. I'm sure we'll see some eagles, but I wonder if we'll see any bighorn sheep or bobcats."

"If we don't, at least we have our own Bob-cat!" Pete said — at which Worthington laughed, Jupiter smiled, and Bob groaned.

"Bighorn sheep used to be plentiful here, but they had to reintroduce a small herd in order to bring them back," Worthington said.

The valley floor fell into deep shadow early as the sun slipped behind the wall of mountains, and the changing light on El Capitan and Half Dome turned them shades of pink and purple. In the gathering dark, Pete sat cross-legged before the burning logs, watching the firelight flicker.

"Isn't this great?" he said. "Maybe tomorrow we can check out our walkie-talkies. I can see it now – Jupe at the top of El Capitan, Bob on the summit of Half Dome – "

"And you asleep in your sleeping bag," Bob said.

All four of them laughed this time.

Jupiter suddenly said, "When we first got here, I was thinking about the elementary school class we took in American history – the one where we learned about all those thousands and thousands of people who left the East during the Gold Rush, with all their belongings in a wagon pulled by horses or oxen. And the people from other countries. People looking for a new start."

"Getting here by boat from somewhere far away," Bob said.

"Every single one of them – except for the Native Americans who were here already – was an immigrant," Jupiter said. "Well, now that I think of it, even the Native Americans were immigrants. Paleontologists now believe their ancestors came to Alaska over a land bridge from Siberia."

As they stared at the flames, Pete thought of his mother, whose ancestors could be traced back to the Spaniards who had come to California seeking the seven cities of gold, and of his father – perhaps descended partly from the Aztecs or the Mayans, but certainly from Spanish conquistadors – whose parents had come to California in search of a new and better life.

"The three of us are perfect examples," Bob said. "We're all Americans, but we're also descendants of people who came to this country looking for freedom, and a new life."

Jupiter nodded. "My great-great-great-great grandfather came over from Wales, where he was a coal miner. The only thing I know about my mother is that she was Serbian."

Pete was surprised to hear this.

"I didn't know your mother was Serbian, Jupe. I thought your parents were killed in Canada!"

"They were," said Jupiter. "But Uncle Titus told me my mother could speak Serbian. He never met her."

Pete said, "Where *is* Serbia, anyway?"

"It's in southern Europe," said Bob. "In

the Balkans."

"Compared to you guys," Pete said, "I'm practically a local. Mexico's a lot closer than Wales or Serbia or China. Of course, my Mom's family came to California from Spain – a long, long time ago."

Worthington cleared his throat.

"I expect you boys think of me as a proper Englishman," he said, "if not from the upper classes."

"Well, not so much in those clothes," Pete said. "But you seem pretty upper class to me. That accent works every time."

"Thank you, Pete," Worthington said. "But I'm a bit more like you boys than you've ever realized."

What could Worthington mean? Pete wondered. Was he part Irish? Or maybe he was Scottish like Mallory MacLeod!

"Though I grew up in Cornwall, my father's parents both came from Shropshire, and my mother was born in Cardiff – in Wales, just like Jupiter's ancestor. But my mother's father was Indian."

Pete felt confused for an instant. "Your grandfather was an *Indian*?"

"I think he means from India, Pete," Jupiter said.

Of course, Pete thought, blushing in the dark.

"Yes," Worthington said. "Jupiter's right. My grandfather was from the Indian subcontinent – from Bengal, actually – which the English colonized and made part of their empire. He was a Lascar – a seaman who served for years on a British merchant ship. When his agreed-upon term of service was finished, he landed in Cardiff and a few years later he married a local girl. Their daughter – my mother – eventually moved to Cornwall with my father."

"Wow!" said Bob. "I've read about Lascars! All three of us knew you looked – well, aside from being really handsome, you looked just a little different from all those English guys we saw in movies."

Worthington laughed. "I'll take that as a compliment, Bob."

"That's how I meant it," Bob said.

In the firelight, Pete tried to look at Worthington through eyes informed with this new knowledge, but he was having a hard time. He still looked – well, just like Worthington.

"Was your grandfather Hindu or Muslim?" Jupiter asked.

"Hindu," said Worthington.

Hindu! thought Pete. That meant he believed in reincarnation! At least, Pete *thought* it did. He felt too shy to ask Worthington just at the moment.

"But here we all are," Jupiter said. "Our families came from all over the world, and yet, somehow, the four of us have made our way here, around this campfire."

"And we seem to really belong here," Bob said.

"I'll buy a double helping of that," said Pete.

Soon after, they let the fire mumble into coals, then the three of them crawled into one tent, while Worthington crawled into the other.

The next day they were up early, and as they were making breakfast, a golden eagle flew above them. Its wing span was enormous, and it was so close that all of them could see its beak, its eyes, and even its talons, and as Pete looked at it, he felt he understood completely why some Native American tribes had had spirit animals – because they had wanted their power and protection.

Not that a golden eagle would be *his* animal, he reflected.

"Hey, Jupe," he said. "That's what *you're* like – a giant bird flying over the earth, looking down on it."

Bob looked up at the eagle and nodded. "Seeing things that other people fail to see," he said. "Oh, no, I just remembered. I have to turn my cellphone back on in case John Chang calls."

He did, and after they finished eating, Worthington went for a walk to stretch his legs, while Bob and Jupiter sat poring over a map they had picked up of the trail system in Yosemite. Pete scanned the sky for more golden eagles. Where they were camped, cell reception was iffy at best, so Pete was surprised when the phone suddenly rang.

Bob flipped it open, turned the volume up, then set it in the middle of the picnic table.

"Hello?" Bob said.

"Is that one of The Three Investigators?" asked an unknown male voice.

"I'm Bob Andrews," Bob said. Pete was fairly certain this must be John Chang, but since he wasn't *quite* certain, he wasn't surprised when Bob said politely – as if he wasn't, either – "How can I help you?"

The man laughed.

"Well, really," he said, "I think it's *I* who can help you – by saving you a lot of wasted time and effort."

"We're not interested in buying

anything," said Bob, while Pete rolled his eyes in exasperation.

"I'm not a salesperson. My name is John Chang. My cousin Isabella has told me she's sending you boys on a wild goose chase after gold."

"I don't understand what you mean," Bob said.

"Of course, I love Isabella dearly, but she's getting on in years now, and lately her obsession with this rumor about a stash of gold seems to have consumed her. I imagine she's hired you boys to find this supposed treasure, and I'm calling to tell you there isn't one. You can spend your time a lot more productively than by coming up to Auburn."

Normally Pete and Bob let Jupiter do the talking in a case like this, but since they were using Bob's cellphone, Bob blurted out, "That's not why she hired us at all. She doesn't believe in the rumors any more than you do. She just wants as much information as she can get about an ancestor of hers who was educated at a one-room schoolhouse. We thought we might take a look at it."

There was a pause on the other end of the line, and when John Chang spoke again, he sounded quite different. Less blustery. Almost sad.

"I seem to be the bearer of a lot of bad news," he said. "Two months ago, the schoolhouse was ransacked by vandals. As the head of the Gold Country Historical Society, I'd been hoping to get the money to conserve it – maybe even turn it into a museum – but some hooligans trashed it. The man who owned it hired a demolition company to raze the rest of the structure. There's nothing there now but a dangerous prospector with a gun. I don't know what would happen if you went anywhere near her."

Pete could hardly believe how weird it was to be having this phone call on a sunny morning in Yosemite Valley. He looked at Bob, who was getting agitated.

"We appreciate your concern, Mr. Chang, but we've made our plans, and we'll be sticking to them. If you'd rather we didn't come and see you when we get to Auburn, just tell us," Bob said.

"No, no," said John Chang, quite hurriedly. "Of course you should come and see me if you're in the area. I know everything there is to know about Li Chang and his schoolteacher, Angus O'Malley. The O'Malley family has fallen on hard times, of course. Angus O'Malley's descendant Connor O'Malley is one of the town's eccentrics – long-haired and wild-looking. He calls himself an artist, but no rational person could think he *is* one."

"Mr. Chang?" interjected Jupiter suddenly. "My name is Jupiter Jones and Bob has just brought me onto this phone call. Isabella mentioned something about Connor O'Malley being interested in the rumors about Li Chang's father being murdered for treasure. Would you confirm that, sir?"

"Good Lord, yes," said John Chang. "He can't shut up about it. Well, if you're determined to come, you'd better tell me where you'll be staying and when you'll be getting here."

Pete could tell that Jupiter didn't want to, but since he saw no way around it, he gave John Chang the information he had asked for.

"I'll see you soon then," John Chang said.

"Yes," said Jupiter. "Goodbye for now."

Bob closed the phone and sat there looking stunned. Pete knew exactly how he felt.

"He clearly called to discourage us from going to the Gold Country," Jupiter said after a moment. "Also, his voice changed completely when you told him that Isabella Chang had suggested we might take a look at the one-room schoolhouse. There's more to this than is immediately apparent."

"That's too bad about the schoolhouse," Pete said.

"It's peculiar, too," Jupiter said. "It stood for how many years? A hundred and fifty or more? And it was just torn down two months ago?"

"Coincidence?" asked Bob.

"In the course of our investigations," Jupiter said, "I've become less and less convinced by coincidences like that one."

"At least he gave us the name of Li Chang's teacher," Bob said. "I couldn't find it anywhere when I was at the library doing research."

"Yes," Jupiter said. "And he also gave us the name of Angus O'Malley's descendant, Connor O'Malley – then did everything he could to make us dislike and distrust the man before we ever met him."

"How did you know this Connor O'Malley might believe in the stash of gold?" Pete asked.

"I didn't," Jupiter said. "A shot in the dark."

"Jupiter's great at getting people to say

more than they think they're saying," Bob said. "Almost as good as he is at playing dumb. When he asked John Chang the question, you were probably still thinking about the curse Rose Chang put on the gold."

"No, I wasn't," Pete said. "I was thinking about that woman with the gun!"

"We'll deal with Annie Oakley when we meet her," Jupiter said. He sounded pleased when he concluded, "I have every expectation that this case will be more exciting and complex than I had reason to believe at first."

"I hope so," Pete said. "At least more exciting than watching Bob take a picture of a poem. Anyway, I'm glad Chang finally called. Now Bob can shut his phone off and forget it, and we can finally go hiking!"

Just then, Worthington came back, and they decided that he should drive to a trailhead about ten miles from camp, and that Pete should take one of the walkie-talkies and hike ahead of the other three far enough so that at least he'd be out of real hearing range when he tested it. He went charging up the trail clutching the walkie-talkie.

"Number One, do you read me?" he said repeatedly until Jupiter got tired of saying "Affirmative."

At a place where a secondary trail cut off, Pete waited for the others. He sat on a granite boulder close to the path, but though the sun was warm on his face and he found himself closing his eyes, he realized as he sat there that, although Bob could shut his phone off, he – Pete – couldn't shut his mind off quite as easily. He found himself thinking about what Bob had said about the curse on the gold. The other night, he'd told his mother about it when he'd gotten home.

"A curse!" his mother had said. "Mother of God! Be careful."

"Well, it doesn't have a curse on it any more," Pete had told her. "It only lasted fifty years and it ran out long ago."

"That's a relief," his mother said. "It's been cleansed."

"Yeah," Pete had said.

"Unlike the Aztec curses," his mother said.

"This was an Irish curse," Pete said.

"Oh, the Irish," his mother said. "They have very weak curses, anyway."

Despite the fact that he knew it wasn't rational, Pete had been glad to hear that. He was still glad, in a way, but he was also a little apprehensive, because when he and the others had come up with their plan to travel to Auburn, they had thought it would be a sort of vacation, but from what John Chang had said, Pete could see that *he*, at least, thought the gold existed. Where there was gold, there was greed, and where there was greed, there was danger.

He opened his eyes again and saw, with some surprise, that two small rodents that looked like very big mice were sitting on a nearby rock regarding him. It seemed they'd never seen anything like him, and their little ears twitched in fascination or fright.

"It's O.K., guys," Pete said soothingly.

When the walkie-talkie squawked, they scurried for safety.

"Second Investigator," Bob's voice said. "Are you there?"

"I'm here," Pete said. "Where are you guys?"

"Jupe got a pebble in his boot and we're stopping so he can get it out," said Bob.

"Well, hurry up!" Pete said. "There are animals here!"

The straggling three showed up about five minutes later.

"You saw animals?" Jupiter asked. "What did you see? A bobcat? A bighorn sheep? A bear?"

"You mean there are still bears here, too?" Pete asked in surprise.

"Black bears, not grizzlies," Jupiter said. "All the grizzlies in California were killed a long time ago. The only grizzlies here these days are on the state flag."

Pete told him about the animals he'd seen.

"They were about this big," he said, holding his hands apart. "Two of them. Like hamsters, only bigger."

"The American pika, no doubt," Jupiter said. "A diurnal herbivore. Very scary."

Pete and Bob smiled. They both liked it when Jupiter made jokes. Pete didn't mention what he'd been thinking about gold and greed and danger. Instead, he said, meeting Jupiter's joke with his own, "If the golden eagle is your spirit animal, maybe the pika is mine!"

Back at camp, they ate supper and made an early night of it. During supper, they got out their binoculars and scanned the surrounding mountains to see if they could catch a glimpse of a bighorn sheep. No luck. The sunset was very pretty, though, and after they said good night to Worthington, they talked about John Chang again when they'd settled in their tent.

The next morning they were off for the four-hour drive to Auburn. On the way, they stopped in Jackson, where Worthington had once worked, to have lunch. Although at one time they'd considered panning for gold at Roaring Camp or even taking a surface tour of the Kennedy Mine, after a day and a half in Yosemite, Jupiter was eager to get going on the case.

Pete could tell that he was still thinking about John Chang, and as they ate, Jupiter said that he wanted to start the investigation by visiting the Gold Country Museum where Isabella Chang had told them the plaques from the one-room schoolhouse were on display.

Still, before they got back in the car, they took a walk around Jackson. The downtown was a combination of old brick buildings and whitewashed wooden ones, some with second story balconies that overhung the sidewalk. As they came around a corner, they stopped.

At the top of a high hill was an imposing white church with a bell tower. Steep concrete steps led up to it, past two enormous cedars on either side of the walk. At the bottom, a graceful wooden arch connected two posts flanked with wing-like side panels and topped with large ball finials. Above the arch, a triangular cornice held an unusual flared cross. On the cornice was written *1894* and *St. Sava Serbian Orthodox Church.*

Pete's mouth almost dropped open. Until the other night Pete had had no idea that Jupiter's mother had been Serbian, and here was a Serbian church, right in Jackson, California. Beyond the wooden arch, on the way to the church itself, was a cemetery with odd names (odd to Pete!) engraved on the gravestones, names like Vasilovich and Marich and Krzic.

"Jupe," he called out, in astonishment. "Now here's a coincidence, if you want to call it that! But I bet my mother would say that our walking by this church was somehow *meant!*"

8

On The Trail of Li Chang

As Jupiter stared at St. Sava's gleaming in the sun, he had to admit that Pete was right. Not that this was somehow *meant*, of course. But it *did* seem quite a coincidence that just days after he'd started wondering about his mother, he was standing before a Serbian church – which seemed a major landmark of the town.

"Boy, some of these gravestones are *old*," Pete said.

"And most of them end with *ic* or *ich*," said Bob. "Here's a whole bunch of Marcovi-ches."

As he glanced at where Bob's finger was pointing, Jupiter saw that many of the grave-stones were clearly modern, and the graveyard was well-tended. For a moment, Jupiter felt dis-oriented and then his brain kicked into gear. Along with all the other people who'd de-scended on this part of California in the middle of the 19th century, Serbians had come. The community must have been founded during the Gold Rush.

"Worthington," he asked. "When you

141

worked here, did you know any Serbians?"

"I didn't know any myself. At least not to know I knew," Worthington said, "although I was aware of the Serbian community."

"Well," Jupiter said. "I doubt any of my relatives are buried here, but I'm gratified to learn something new about the years that lie at the heart of our current case. Nevertheless, there's no time to investigate this further now. The day is flying by, and it's time we got going."

They climbed into the Land Rover and were soon on their way. Although they had reservations to stay in a cabin outside of Auburn that night, it was still just the middle of the day, and Jupiter wanted to see what Li Chang had written on his graduation plaque. He hoped it would reveal something significant about its writer.

For that reason, as they wound their way north Jupiter found himself thinking about the characters they had encountered so far. First, Isabella Chang – hardworking, self-directed – a person of wide-ranging knowledge, to whom education itself had always been the greatest good.

Next, her distant cousin John Chang – a man who had made his money developing real estate, but who was also the head of the Gold Country Historical Society. Although a man like that might be seeking to balance his personal success with his civic responsibility, his phone call to The Three Investigators had been such a blatant attempt to intimidate them that Jupiter was almost certain John Chang wasn't what he tried to seem.

Then there was Li Chang – a total unknown who Jupiter hoped to start to get to know by reading a poem he had written when he was the same age Jupiter, Pete, and Bob were now. It was lucky the plaques had been taken out of the Abecedarian Academy before it was torn down, Jupiter thought.

Although the schoolhouse where Li Chang had studied had been of interest before, now that it was gone, Jupiter found himself fascinated by it. After all, he reasoned, it was one sort of coincidence to encounter a Serbian church in the town of Jackson, and another entirely to find that the building they'd just heard about from Isabella Chang had so recently been destroyed.

He could recognize that feeling he got when his mind was fully engaged and the pieces of the puzzle were beginning to assemble – as though he, like the Land Rover, had been put into a higher gear. A humming in the engine of his mind, a heightened clarity in everything he saw and heard.

An hour later they were in Auburn – back in the foothills of the Sierras but further north. To the east, the boys could occasionally catch glimpses of snowcapped peaks. The North Fork of the American River ran through a deep canyon, then down to Folsom Lake, which the boys had skirted earlier, and the hills were dotted with olive groves. With help from the GPS, Worthington found the Gold Country Historical Museum on the outskirts of town.

It was housed in a building that dated from the late 1800s but had a modern addition of steel and glass in the back. As soon as the boys entered, they were greeted by an older woman who sat behind a curved wood bar that looked as though it had its own history behind it.

"Hello, boys," the woman said. "Hot enough for you today?"

"It's nice and cool in here," Pete said.

"I wonder if you can help us," Jupiter said. "We heard that you have a collection of plaques from a one-room schoolhouse east of Auburn. They were made by the best students in each class when they graduated from eighth

144

grade."

The woman brightened. "Yes, indeed," she said. "We plan to restore them as best we can when we have the funds. They're a little the worse for wear, I'm afraid, but they're hanging in the small room on the left at the top of the stairs." She pointed to a steep staircase in the older part of the building.

The room was indeed quite small, with a display case in the middle that contained old ink bottles, some rusted pen nibs, a moth-eaten ancient backpack, and a slate that one of the students must have written on with chalk. About twenty plaques had been hung around the room, and Jupiter began to study them with interest.

Constructed of pine boards nailed together and rounded at the top and bottom, they were mostly about a foot and a half wide and two feet high. Some of the plaques had warped a little, and the writing had faded on all of them, but with one or two exceptions, the ink was still quite readable. Jupiter was carefully making his way around the room when he heard Bob shout, "Jupe! Over here!"

Jupiter and Pete hurried to Bob's side and all three stared at what was clearly the longest and most complicated poem ever written by a graduating student at the school.

Because of the message's length, the faded print was very small. Some words were hard to decipher. Jupiter took the magnifying glass from his backpack.

Passing it slowly over the letters, he read:

Our parents came to this country
From many other lands.
They sought to grow and flourish
Through working with minds and hands.

Our parents came to this country,
Looking for things to build.
They saw new peaks and valleys,
They dug in the earth for gilt.

Some of our parents prospered,
Some of our parents died,
But all of them bequeathed us
A gift that will abide.

Our parents gave us freedom
To be what we could be.
They also gave us schoolbooks,
since knowledge should always be free.

Athena, Goddess of Wisdom,

I take you away today
To ride on my left shoulder
And guide me along my way.

Already you have taught me
That though men may die for greed –
The greediness of others –
The greatest gold is that we read.

Already you have taught me
That though anyone may be killed,
Words, which last forever,
Are the heart of life, distilled.

~ Li Chang

"Wow!" Pete said. "That's pretty good for someone our age."

"I can see why Li Chang was the school's star pupil," Bob said. "And he really had something he wanted to say!"

Jupiter nodded. He read Li Chang's message a number of times, lingering over various phrases. His heart beat faster as he read the poem as a kind of puzzle. The Three Investigators had had a number of cases which revolved around written puzzles – although they'd never had one in which the puzzle had been written by accident, so to speak.

"Yes," Jupiter said to Bob. "In fact, he seems to have said a good deal more than it looks like he said. You told us that Li Chang's father was killed when Li was just thirteen. He was still a student of Angus O'Malley's then, and when he wrote this poem, the death of his father must have been very much on his mind."

"What do you mean?" Pete asked.

Jupiter pointed to the beginning of the poem. "These first eight lines," he said, "could refer to just about anyone. They're about the shared experience of the immigrants who came to California during the gold rush, searching for a new life. Look at how Li Chang keeps saying 'our.' He's not speaking personally."

"You're right," Bob said. "And the eight lines after that are about the schoolhouse — about how the students' parents thought education was very important."

"Yes," Jupiter said. "That's clear. But do you see what happens after that?" Jupiter asked.

"He starts talking to Athena," Pete said.

"Correct," Jupiter said.

"The goddess of wisdom," Pete added.

"An important Greek god," said Jupiter. "I believe she may have also been the goddess of justice. But even more important is the fact that Li Chang starts talking personally. He's no longer talking about 'we.' He's talking about 'I'."

Jupiter looked from Bob to Pete and went on. "Another way to put it would be to say that in the beginning, he's addressing the poem to a general audience – it could be anyone. But then Li Chang's attention shifts, and he starts, for some reason I cannot yet deduce, to speak directly to Athena."

"But how can a Greek goddess ride on Li Chang's shoulder?" Pete asked.

"That," Jupiter admitted, "I do not know. Nevertheless, the tone of the poem shifts from a recitation of facts to something much more personal. It's interesting that, in the last two stanzas, Li Chang uses words like 'die' and 'killed'."

"Well," Bob said. "You just said that Li Chang's father was murdered not long before he wrote this poem. That would explain it."

"Yes," Jupiter said. "But it doesn't explain the words 'greed' and 'gold'. Isabella Chang told us that her ancestor was murdered because he was Chinese, and dismissed out of hand any suggestion that he was murdered for his gold. But you told us that when Li Chang's mother was interviewed by a reporter for the Auburn *Journal,* she said the murderer himself was Chinese. Both her report to the paper and the ending of Li's poem suggest that greed – not hatred – was the actual motive for the killing."

"I agree with you, Jupe," Bob said. "After all, if Li believed his father died at the hands of people who hated him because he was Chinese, he would have written a very different kind of poem. It might have started out the same, but by the end, he would have been writing about *that.* Instead, he compares one kind of treasure – the knowledge found in books – with the kind that men will kill for."

"I *knew* there was really some gold!" Pete said.

"Don't get carried away, Pete," Bob said. "Even if it's true that Li Chang's father was killed for his gold, it's long gone. The killer or killers would have spent it; they wouldn't have hidden it."

Although Jupiter felt almost certain Bob was right, he couldn't help hoping that he was wrong. The idea of finding something of great value with little work obviously held enormous appeal to human beings. Why else would so many thousands of people – three hundred

thousand, Isabella Chang had told them −
have abandoned their lives and hurried to California on the off-chance that they could dig in
the dirt and become very rich?

He thought about this as Bob took a picture of Li Chang's plaque with his cellphone.

"Sadly, I think Bob's right, Pete," Jupiter
said. "Whatever gold there might have been is
probably long gone. But at least Li Chang
himself is beginning to come into focus."

Now it was time to see what they could
find out about the building where Li and his
mother − and later Li and his wife − had their
laundry. Jupiter hadn't known if they'd have
time to look for this building today, but they
did.

Though Pete looked gloomy at Jupiter's
comment about the gold, by the time the boys
left the museum, he had recovered his good
spirits.

Worthington was waiting for them in the
parking lot.

"Worthington!" Pete said excitedly.
"Jupe thinks there might have been a stash of
gold once! And I bet we can find it, if it's still
here somewhere!"

"Indeed?" said Worthington. "That
would be a rare event!" He got them on the

road, maneuvering the Land Rover back through the center of Auburn and past the stately Placer County Courthouse with its copper-topped cupola, down the steep hill to Old Town. It, too, seemed to be a museum these days.

"It's funny that it's called Old Town," Pete said.

Jupiter understood what Pete meant. Though the area was small – only a few blocks of buildings at the base of wide steep curved roads – it was clearly now a tourist destination, teeming with cars and pedestrians. Banners hung from shops and restaurants. Still, behind the commercial exteriors, Jupiter could see the bones of the past – the original brick storefronts with their signature second-story balconies. It had been a small sheltered spot, away from the wildness of the gold camps.

"Still, it *is* the original town," Bob said. "And I like the old fire station. Which doesn't seem to be used any more."

Worthington parked the Land Rover and told the boys he'd be taking a walk; if they needed him, he'd be in the small park on the edge of Old Town – the one with the large rough statue of a gold miner. He pointed to it and strode off.

Bob had already programmed into the GPS the address of the building in which Li Chang's laundry had once been, but he suddenly switched it off.

"You know," he said to Jupiter. "It'd be pretty easy to get addicted to this device. I think we should find the building on our own."

Jupiter agreed. The building they were looking for was on Sacramento Street, and as they walked toward it, instead of staring at a small hand-held device, they stared at the buildings and storefronts – each with a number on its side. After passing an antique shop and a jeweler specializing in old silver and turquoise, they found the building they were looking for. The sign out front read "Small's Café."

Pete and Bob were thrilled.

"It's still here!" Bob said.

"We're lucky," Jupiter said. "The schoolhouse is gone and so many of these old buildings have been torn down."

He'd seen evidence of that even here, in Auburn's Old Town, where new construction was everywhere. But as he stared up at the pale red brick façades, re-pointed and cleaned but obviously old, he guessed that this block of buildings dated from the 1800s, and that, at one time, the cement sidewalk they were standing on had been wooden planks raised above the mud.

Jupiter led the way inside. The place was long and narrow; a wooden bar at the back had a small line of customers waiting for coffee and sandwiches, but the café was largely empty; it was getting close to the end of the working day. Small metal tables with wide-backed metal chairs filled the room, and just a few customers remained, drinking, eating, and talking quietly.

Though the café's front was bright with natural light from the big glass windows on Sacramento Street, the back was dim. Both side walls were brick, and they were crowded with antiques and mementoes – framed photos of Auburn and Old Town in earlier days, the shallow steeply sloped pans in which the pros-pectors had swirled river rocks and sand, hop-ing for a nugget, a double-bladed miner's pick, an assayer's scale with an elongated figure of a miner serving as its central post, a wooden yoke for cattle, and –

"Holy moly!" Pete said.

"You can say that again," Bob said. Pete remained silent, staring, along with Jupiter and Bob, at a copy of the Talisman Against Demons now hanging in the Jones Salvage

Yard.

"Talk about coincidence!" Pete said.

Jupiter felt that heightened sense of excitement again. Although this obviously *was* simply coincidence, it certainly seemed significant just now. He stared at the talisman hanging, shadowed, against the hard brick of the wall, and noted the ways it differed from the one his uncle had brought home not even a week ago.

That one was printed on very thin metal – modern metal, Jupiter thought – while the one on the wall before him looked much older, and was canvas stretched on a wooden frame. Though its aspect was the same, it seemed a bit smaller.

Something else was different – Jupiter couldn't put his finger on it – but at least he was sure that the image of the Chinese man was identical. Swathed in his saffron robe, he held a fat green sword and the swirl of motion created by the man's eyebrows, mustache, beard and hair was the same. Jupiter concluded that both the one on canvas and the one on metal were copies made from an original the boys had never seen.

"I wonder where it came from," Bob said.

"Maybe we can ask someone who works here," Jupiter said. "Why don't you and Pete grab a table, and I'll get us some drinks."

"If they have root beer – " Pete said.

Jupiter waited in line while the man behind the wooden bar made a cappuccino for a tall well-dressed woman in red high heels. The man had bushy eyebrows and a bushy beard.

"There you are," he said to the woman. He smiled broadly. His eyes were blue, with crinkles in the corners. Jupiter guessed he was in his fifties.

The woman paid him and turned away and Jupiter moved up to the bar, then ordered two Cokes and a root beer.

"I've never been in here before," he said. "Do you know the history of that print over there?" He turned and pointed in the direction of the talisman.

"You mean Uncle Kepa?" the man asked and laughed. "Kepa means 'terrible' in Mandarin, I understand."

"My uncle owns a salvage yard near Los Angeles," Jupiter said, "and just last week he came back with a bunch of Chinese talismans – one of which was a copy of this one. Or this one is a copy of that one."

"They're both copies, I think," the man

said. "By the way, I'm Gordon Small and this is my café."

Jupiter took out a Three Investigators card and handed it to the man.

"The Three Investigators!" he said. "So you're investigating my building?"

"Actually," Jupiter said. "We're investigating the history of a man by the name of Li Chang. We believe he owned a laundry and dry goods store at this location."

"Now that is very interesting," Mr. Small said. "Not many people know about the laundry any more."

He picked up the tray with the drinks on it and carried them to the table, where Jupiter introduced him to Pete and Bob – hoping that Mr. Small's comment about Li Chang's laundry meant that he himself *did* know about it.

When Mr. Small pulled up a chair and sat down, Jupiter asked him.

"Most of the Chinese families who lived here at that time have moved away," Mr. Small said. "If I've got my dates right, Li Chang died more than a hundred years ago – though his widow kept the laundry going well into the 1930s. After that, another family ran it until the early 1960s, and after that, it was turned into a dry cleaners. It was still a dry cleaners when I bought it, ten years ago, and turned it into a café."

"You seem to have been extremely successful," Jupiter said.

"Thank you!" Mr. Small said. "I certainly like to think so!"

"Now, about Li Chang – " Jupiter said.

"I wish I knew more about him," Mr. Small said. "Very successful with the laundry. Well-educated, with a wide range of knowledge. Knew Greek, from what I can gather. Died in the flu epidemic of 1918. I found the talisman in the upper attic."

Jupiter sat up straight. "The talisman came from the attic of this building?"

"Why yes," Mr. Small said. "And some other things as well. When you look at the storefront you can see there are two floors. This first floor I made into the café and the second floor is the apartment where I live. But one day I was staring up at the second story windows and I realized that the roof peak was higher than I would have expected it to be – that there would logically be some space up there.

"So I started looking up at the ceiling of my apartment, and sure enough I found a trapdoor that had been plastered over. Most of what you see on the walls here was up in the attic. The talisman fascinated me, so I did some research. Turns out it was originally painted in about 1904 in San Francisco by a Chinese artist. There seem to have been a lot of demons in San Francisco – ” Mr. Small laughed heartily, “ – because many copies were made – among them this one, and maybe the one your uncle found.”

“Did you find any papers in the attic?” Bob asked. “A notebook or a journal? Anything like that?”

Mr. Small pointed to several objects on the walls of the café. “No papers, but a few other interesting objects. Heaven knows what Li Chang was doing with an oxen yoke or a miner’s pick or an assayer's scale. Maybe he panned for gold; almost everyone did.

“There was one other thing – quite fascinating, really. A Greek/English primer printed in 1870. When you opened it, there was Greek on the left-hand page and the English translation of the Greek on the right-hand page.

“An inscription on the flyleaf read 'To Li Chang, the best student in the class of 1873. With congratulations.' It was written in careful calligraphy and signed with some initials. The book was called *Athena, Goddess of Wisdom.*”

"Yikes," Pete said in a whisper. Bob whooped loudly, and in the back of Jupiter's mind puzzle pieces began to lock in place.

"Do you still have the book?" he asked Mr. Small.

"You boys seem very excited," Gordon Small said.

"Yes, indeed," Jupiter told him. "We've encountered the book before."

"Well, I expect it was a pretty common primer back then."

"Perhaps," said Jupiter, "but that isn't why we know about it. We've just been studying a poem Li Chang wrote when he graduated from eighth grade. We couldn't imagine why he started talking to the Greek goddess Athena halfway through it, but now we can see that he was referring – at least in part – to the book which was his graduation prize. Do you still have the book?" he asked again.

"I thought it was so important to the history of the area that I gave it to the Gold Country Museum when it opened three years ago," said Mr. Small. "I also arranged for the plaques to be rescued from the old schoolhouse and given to the museum before a local real estate developer bought the land the schoolhouse was on."

Although he was certain he already knew the answer, Jupiter asked, "Was the name of the real estate developer John Chang?"

"You've heard of him?" asked Gordon Small.

"Yes," Jupiter said. "We'll have to go back to the museum and ask to see the book," he added to Pete and Bob. "It wasn't in the room with the wooden plaques."

All of a sudden, the door of the café flew open and a man burst in. He was wild-eyed and wild-haired; he was breathing hard and his clothes and hair were streaked with paint, smears of red and blue, umber and white. His voice was harsh and agitated.

"Gordon," he said. "You've got to help me! A fire's started in the canyon, and there's a great horned owl that needs our help!" Although Jupiter was as startled as the rest of them, he was also quite intrigued.

9

Athena, Goddess of Wisdom

Bob jumped to his feet and stood next to Pete, alarmed by the new arrival's urgency and agitation. Up until the time he arrived in the café – and ever since the boys had spotted the Chinese talisman – Bob had actually been thinking about Mallory MacLeod.

Of course, he'd also been listening to Jupiter talk to Mr. Small, but when he'd seen the Chinese man swathed in his saffron robe, his mind had gone back to the moment when Mallory had biked into the Salvage Yard. She'd stood and stared up at the talismans swaying gently in the breeze.

Now, Bob was wrenched from this memory by the sudden intrusion into the café.

"Connor!" Mr. Small said. "A fire! Where in the canyon?"

"At a picnic area near the American River. But the fire department has been alerted and – well, you can hear the sirens now," he said as Bob heard a perfect cacophony in the distance.

The man was out of breath and had a

hard time getting his story out.

"Still, that isn't the point. At the soccer fields. That red plastic netting?" He coughed and cleared his throat.

"Would you like some root beer?" Pete asked.

The man looked grateful, took the glass, and upended it.

"A great horned owl," he said again. "Tangled in the netting, and he's frantic to get loose. He's obviously been there all day long. He's going to hurt himself. I was there when I saw the tendrils of smoke below me and called the fire department, but you and I have got to cut the owl free."

He bent over and took a very deep breath. "You hold him, I'll cut the netting. Gordon, hurry up." He grabbed Mr. Small by the arm and started pulling him toward the door.

"Connor," Mr. Small said. "I'm the only one here. I can't go with you now."

"Oh, no!" the man said.

"We can help you, sir," Jupiter said.

"Yes," Pete added. "We have a lot of experience with animals."

This wasn't strictly true. None of the boys had pets, and although the Rocky Beach

Elementary School had had a sort of petting zoo out back, the animals they had taken care of had been domestic, not frantic wild ones.

Still, Bob could understand why Pete had said what he'd said. He and Jupiter wanted to help, and Bob did, too.

"Boys, this is my friend Connor O'Malley," said Gordon Small. "You can tell from the way he looks that he's a painter. A very good one. And an animal lover. He and I have rescued a coyote, three raccoons, and several birds. But the three of you can assist him today."

Connor O'Malley! Bob thought. That was the artist John Chang had mentioned as being a descendant of Li Chang's schoolteacher.

"Come on, then!" said Mr. O'Malley. "I've got my car out front. We can go in that."

"You'd better call Worthington first," Jupiter said to Bob.

Bob whipped out his phone and punched Worthington's number. When the call went straight to voicemail, Bob was so startled he hung up without leaving a message.

"He's not answering," Bob said.

"Mr. Small?" Jupiter said. "Our friend Worthington will come looking for us soon, I'm sure. He's a tall man about your age, wearing blue jeans and hiking boots. Tell him we'll be back as soon as we can. Also, if you wouldn't mind, give him this."

He thrust his walkie-talkie at Mr. Small. "His phone may not be working. If not, he can contact us this way."

"I'll tell him, young man," said Mr. Small.

Bob accompanied Mr. O'Malley out onto the sidewalk, quickly followed by Pete and Jupe.

"Now, boys," Mr. O'Malley said, as they all piled into his battered old sedan. "Buckle up!" He pulled away from the curb – almost hitting a parked car in his haste – swerved around another car and got onto the interstate, which ran right through Auburn. Although Bob had liked the man on sight, he found his driving a bit unnerving.

"What should I call you?" the artist asked. As they sped along, the boys introduced themselves.

"I was taking a break from my latest painting," Mr. O'Malley said. "I like to walk the trails near the soccer fields. That's when I found the owl."

"How did he get entangled in the net?"

Jupiter asked.

"I have no idea," Mr. O'Malley said. "Perhaps he was swooping down to catch a mouse or vole. From above, I expect the netting is invisible."

A few miles later, they took an exit, stopped at a traffic light, and then wound down a road that led to the Recreation Park. Before they took the exit, Bob saw a sign for the town of Grass Valley. Mallory MacLeod was probably there now, at the Scottish music camp. He wondered if she would call him.

Mr. O'Malley paid no attention to the parking lot and drove straight across the grass, skidding to a stop before a length of red plastic netting. Bob could see the netting had been stretched along one side of the soccer fields to keep any stray balls from tumbling into the ravine that plunged away not far from the edge of the fields. As Bob climbed out of the car, he saw a plume of white smoke rising into the air from the ravine.

The great horned owl hung in the netting, caught by his wings and talons. He was slightly larger than a football, and Bob could see his horns – the tufted feathers on each side of his head – as well as his curved beak and his large yellow eyes, grave and staring, with their fixed black pupils. The bird was exhausted and had obviously entangled himself further as he'd struggled to get free.

Mr. O'Malley took some leather gloves from the trunk and hurried over to the owl, who glared at him and began to struggle again.

"That's O.K., big fella," Mr. O'Malley said. He turned to the boys. "I'm afraid he's been here since last night. Owls, as you probably know, are nocturnal."

The owl was impressive in every way to Bob; in spite of his situation, he had great dignity, and a fierce intelligence gleamed from his eyes.

"I'll hold him," Pete said.

Bob smiled. Pete might be superstitious and have abstract fears, but when the moment demanded it, you could always count on Pete.

Jupiter reached in his pocket and pulled out his Swiss Army knife. "And I can use the scissors on my knife to cut the netting."

"That's great!" Mr. O'Malley said. "I'll pull the netting free as you cut and get it away from him as quick as I can."

Pete put on the leather gloves and approached the owl with caution.

"Careful how you hold him," Mr.

O'Malley said. "Make sure you don't hurt his wings."

As Bob watched, the owl's eyes seemed to grow larger, but Pete didn't flinch. He pushed up against the netting, wrapped his arm around the owl and drew him close to his chest so the bird couldn't move. The owl's talons settled on Pete's wrist and his head jerked, trying to bite, but Pete held the bird firmly as Jupiter began to cut the red netting loose. The owl's head darted at Jupiter's hands, but he pulled away in time.

"Good lads," Mr. O'Malley said. "Good lads." He was pulling the netting away as quickly as Jupiter could cut it.

Bob was filled with admiration at Pete's courage and the careful way Jupiter tackled the task at hand.

When Jupiter cut the last bit of netting free, Pete stepped away from the fence, still holding the owl – who now wrestled in his arms and bit at his hands. But the job was almost done. Mr. O'Malley skillfully unwrapped the last bits of netting still caught in the owl's wings and talons.

"O.K.," Pete said. "Stand back."

Gently he set the bird on the ground. At first it seemed as if one of its wings might have been hurt, but all of a sudden it spread them wide and flapped them hard, rising in the air to a height of ten feet before he glided off, down into the ravine. The boys spontaneously began to applaud and whoop.

"Wow!" Bob said. "Pete, you were great!"

Pete took off the gloves he'd been wearing. "Yikes!" he said. "Those claws and beak were sharp." Bob looked down at Pete's hands. The talons had punctured the gloves and scratched Pete's skin.

"Did he bite you?" Mr. O'Malley asked.

"He tried," Pete said. "He was more scared than I was, though. Still, no matter how scared he was, he was brave. Maybe, deep down, he knew I wouldn't hurt him."

"Courage is holding steady even when you're scared," Mr. O'Malley said.

Jupiter agreed. "Pete is our champion," he said. "We can always rely on him."

Bob was startled when his walkie-talkie squawked, crackling with static. Jupiter and Pete crowded around as Worthington's voice came over the device. He sounded very concerned, and the boys quickly filled him in on what had happened. Mr. O'Malley assured Worthington he'd bring the boys back to Old

Town immediately. The four of them got into O'Malley's sedan and were soon on their way.

"Tell me about yourselves, boys," Mr. O'Malley said. "I haven't seen you before, and I suspect you're not from these parts."

The boys were so fired up from all that had happened that they kept stepping on one another's explanations. Bob ended up telling the man what had brought them to Auburn. "You might even be part of the story," he said. "Li Chang was taught by Angus O'Malley, an Irish schoolteacher, who I think you might be descended from."

"Yes, indeed," Connor O'Malley said with a big grin. "Old Angus was my grandfather, with a number of 'greats' attached. I can never remember how many."

"Which means," Jupiter said, "that in a very distant way you're also related to Li Chang — because Angus O'Malley was Li Chang's mother's cousin."

"Yes," Connor said. "I guess that's right."

Bob could see that Pete was practically squirming in his seat — a sure sign that he had something to say, but he wasn't sure if he should say it.

He said it anyway.

"We also heard you think that Li Chang's father was killed for a stash of gold," he finally blurted out. "And that maybe that stash is still hidden somewhere."

"Pete!" Jupiter said.

"Well, he did tell us!" Pete said.

Connor O'Malley laughed. "That would be John Chang, no doubt," he said. "If I were you, I wouldn't believe everything he tells you. He's a real estate developer, and as far as I can see, they're all liars. As for the rumors about the gold, I'm a perfect agnostic. Maybe the rumors are true and maybe they're not. I have no real opinion."

They were soon in Old Town. Worthington had moved the Land Rover so that it was parked in front of Small's Café, and he stood there in the shade of the awning, his hands behind his back. As Connor pulled up, Gordon Small was turning the sign to CLOSED and locking the café's door. The boys told Worthington about their adventure in great detail while Connor assured his friend that the owl had been rescued.

"Owl's well that ends well," Mr. Small said, and everybody groaned. "And you'll be glad to hear that the fire in the canyon was small and quickly contained. I heard on the public scanner that it's out now."

"It was another close call," Connor said.

"Yes," said Mr. Small. "Thank heavens you reported it when you did. They don't call them wildfires for nothing."

"All I can say is I'm glad I met The Three Investigators," Connor said. "As a small gesture of thanks, I'd like to show you boys my studio. That is, if you're interested."

"You should go," Gordon Small said. "His work is fascinating, and besides, his studio is in the old Auburn library."

"Isabella Chang told us about that," Bob reminded Jupiter and Pete. "The building became an arts center when the town built a more modern library." After all the research he had done about Carnegie Libraries, Bob would have wanted to see it even if it hadn't been home to artists' studios now.

"Let's go!" Jupiter said.

The boys got into the Land Rover with Worthington and followed Connor O'Malley through Auburn to the old Carnegie Library on Almond Street. It had been built on the side of a gently sloping hill so it looked much bigger and more impressive than the buildings to its left and right.

The lower story had been constructed of

concrete and was mostly above ground, so to get to the main floor you had to ascend a flight of steps and pass between a set of architectural columns on either side of the entrance. The upper half of the building was built of white brick and seemed to Bob to float in the simmering heat of late afternoon. Carved in the stone at the top were the words AUBURN PUBLIC LIBRARY, while underneath that, on the lintel, were the words FREE TO ALL.

Bob stopped and stared at the words, remembering the photograph he'd found online of Li Chang's gravestone. FREE TO ALL had been engraved on the stone as well – probably, Bob thought, because of how important education and books had been to Li Chang. He hadn't shown the others the photograph of the gravestone yet; he'd have to remember to show it to them that evening.

"Thank heavens for Andrew Carnegie," Connor O'Malley said.

"Yes," Bob said. "Isabella Chang told us he thought people should spend the first third of their lives getting as much education as they could, the second third making as much money as they could, and the last third giving it all away to worthwhile causes."

Connor O'Malley laughed. "Like studios

for starving artists," he said.

"Though, of course," Jupiter said, "that was not his original intention."

Connor took all four of them inside and put his finger to his lips in the universal sign that they should be quiet.

"I don't know who's still working today," he whispered, "but we all try to respect one another."

As they followed Connor, Bob could see that the building had not been well-maintained since it had changed from a library to an arts center. Ironically, the walls and window trim needed painting, and there were places where the floor squeaked.

"Mr. O'Malley," he said in a hushed voice. "Did you know this building when it was still a library?"

"Of course," Connor said. "I grew up in Auburn. Though I have to admit, I was never much of a reader. By the way, please call me Connor."

Connor's studio was on the ground floor in the back right-hand corner. It was as disheveled as Connor himself. Tubes of paint, jars full of brushes, and smeared rags covered every horizontal surface. An office chair on casters had been pushed to the side. On a stand-alone bulletin board, Connor had pinned five pieces of paper. Each held a single circle subtly different from the others. When Bob looked closer, he saw they were different versions of what seemed to be a logo for a business called Sierra Adventure Outfitters. Blues and browns predominated; there were stylized mountains and clouds. One featured what looked like a mountain lion.

"Ah," Connor said. "You've discovered my secret."

"What secret?" Bob said.

"I'd love to make a living just painting my pictures," Connor said, "but I'm too fond of eating. I have a sideline as a graphic artist. I design brochures and logos, that sort of thing. It pays the bills. But this is what I'm proud of."

He pointed to the half-finished canvases hung on the walls; others were stacked under a window. The painting Connor was working on stood on an easel in the middle of the workspace. The place smelled of turpentine and mineral spirits.

Bob walked across to look more closely at some of Connor's work. What had looked from a distance like a series of whitish rectangles appeared on closer inspection to be overlapping envelopes, with handwritten addresses and ornate stamps. They were meticulous and exact in their details − the exact opposite of Connor himself. Bob supposed everyone was made up of contradictions − which was what made them interesting, he thought.

"As you can see," Connor told the boys, "I'm obsessed with old-fashioned mail. I remember how exciting it was when I was a boy and a letter arrived. Now the postman brings only bills and catalogues. E-mail has swept our lettered past away."

Bob thought about this. He'd grown up with e-mail and although from time to time he'd gotten a holiday card in the mail, they'd been few and far between.

"Look at how much you could tell about the sender," Connor went on. "The choice of stamp and envelope, the way the address was written. I've copied them exactly."

"Copied?" Jupiter asked.

"Yes," Connor said. "I inherited several boxes of old family letters, and one day I went through them and picked out the most interesting ones. I've been doing a series of paintings."

"Jupe, look at this!" Pete said.

He was hunkered down by the stacked paintings. Bob and Jupiter joined him, and Bob was stunned to see that the envelope in the center of one of the finished canvases – browned at the edges and a bit rumpled – was addressed to Angus O'Malley.

Jupiter stood up quickly, holding the canvas.

"This envelope," he said, "is addressed to Li Chang's teacher, your ancestor Angus. Do you still have the letter that was inside it?"

"I should," Connor said. "I copied the envelopes on my color copier, to paint from, but afterwards I put the letters back. They're at my house." He looked quite sheepish. "I told you I wasn't much of a reader. I'm much more visual and tactile. I'm ashamed to admit I was more interested in the packages the letters came in – which are like works of art to me – than in the letters themselves. I've never read them. But you're more than welcome to come to my house to look through the ones I've got. Maybe tomorrow?"

"That would be great, Mr. O'Malley. Uh, Connor," Jupiter said. "Thanks a million."

"I'm sorry," Worthington said to Connor, "but these boys must be famished and I think I should get them to the place we're staying tonight."

"Of course," Connor said. "I'll see you tomorrow then. Say around noon? I'll try to remember to be home!"

Bob was happy Worthington had spoken up, and happy to be heading to a place where he could eat and go to sleep. Worthington found Highway 49 and followed it on its twisting route down into the American River canyon, over the clear rushing river, and up the steep winding road on the other side.

They found the Sighing Pines Campground and Cabins a few miles further on, about seven miles from Auburn, on the way to Cool. Off to either side of the highway, in the distance, there were hills and gullies, places where the land fell sharply off, probably leading to creeks or ponds. Worthington pulled into the dust and gravel parking lot and Jupiter led the way to the office − a small rustic cabin with a California flag flying from the roof.

The boy who checked them in wasn't much older than they were, Bob thought. He was tall, and thin, and earnest, with a shock of hair as bleached as the summer grass. It turned out he'd grown up in Cool, had just graduated from Golden Sierra High, and was off to Chico State in the fall.

His name was Randy, and he knew where the old schoolhouse had been.

"I used to play there when I was a kid,"

he told them. "Me and my friends. It's not far from a creek where we used to pan for gold. Never found any to speak of, though there are some old timers out there who still have claims."

"Did you ever meet any?" Pete asked.

"We got to know a Grizzly Adams-type guy who took us under his wing. We'd bring him cigarettes we snitched and cans of pork and beans and he'd tell us where we'd strike it rich. Never happened, of course. This was about five, six years ago, and the schoolhouse was still standing then. Me and my friends used to sneak in through an unlocked window."

The boy gave Jupiter the key to Number 5 and pointed the way. Number 5 was a rustic cabin of rough-sawn wood, with a front porch roof supported by two strong posts, just like the office of the Salvage Yard. From a small living area with a well-worn sofa, a wooden table and chairs, and a kitchenette, you could get to the bedrooms and bathroom. One of the bedrooms had a double bed, the other had bunk beds and an additional single.

"Pretty good for what we're paying," Bob said.

"I get the double!" Pete yelled and went in to bounce on the springs. "Only kidding,

Worthington!"

They quickly unpacked and then the boys made soup and sandwiches and set the table for the four of them. Worthington seemed even hungrier than they were, and while they ate, Jupiter filled him in on what they'd discovered before Connor O'Malley had burst into Gordon Small's café.

Worthington listened with interest while they told him about the poem Li Chang had written, its mention of Athena, Goddess of Wisdom, and their subsequent discovery that this referred in part to the Greek/English primer Li had gotten as a graduation prize.

"Tomorrow," Jupiter said, "after we visit Mr. O'Malley, we need to get back to the museum so we can look at Li Chang's copy of the book. Maybe we can also take a look at the site where the one-room schoolhouse stood."

"Very exciting," Worthington said. "It seems you boys are closing in on your target. But Athena was not only the goddess of wisdom. She was also the goddess of inspiration, art, and civilization. And you'll be interested, Pete, to hear that she must have been beside you earlier today, because she is also the goddess of courage, and her sacred animal is an owl known as the Owl of Athena."

"Whoa!" Pete said. "No way!"

"Cultures all over the world have venerated owls, or thought of them as special, or attached superstitions to them," Worthington said. "Before we left Rocky Beach, I was reading about the Native Americans who once inhabited the Sierras. According to my reading, they believed that great horned owls accompanied the souls of the dead to the afterlife."

"Great horned owls like the one we rescued?" Pete said in wonder – just as Bob remembered the photograph of Li Chang's gravestone.

"Wait a minute," he said.

He rifled through one of his research folders and found the photo.

"Jupiter," he said. "Can you get the magnifying glass?"

Jupiter rummaged in his backpack and came up with the glass. Using it to study the gravestone, the three boys huddled together. Bob had been right in his guess; the tiny, blurry carving of what seemed to be some sort of bird or animal riding on the top of the "Li" section of Li Chang's name was almost certainly an owl. Not a great horned owl – at least Bob didn't think so – but, still, an owl of some kind.

"Yikes!" Pete said. "And it also says

FREE TO ALL. Just like the motto above the door of the library."

"What do you think?" Bob asked Jupiter.

"Worthington," Jupiter said. "Will you look at this please?"

Worthington took the magnifying glass and bent close over the photograph.

"I would say," he told the boys, "that what you have here, on this gravestone, is nothing other than an Owl of Athena."

"O.K.," Pete said. "I've had enough!"

"Enough what?" Bob asked.

"Enough coincidence!" Pete said. "At first I thought all those coincidences piling up were kind of neat. But now they're giving me the creeps. I won't be able to sleep tonight."

"Sure you will," Bob said. "Unless you hear an owl hooting."

"Very funny," Pete said.

"All those coincidences?" Jupiter asked. "Remember Li Chang's poem? When he suggested Athena rode on his shoulder? He must have been thinking of the owl. I have a feeling that all of this is leading us in the right direction!"

Bob thought so, too, but he wished he could see the case's conclusion, just to be sure. He liked that satisfying feeling of knowing how things turned out. After all, some coincidences were significant and others were just random, and in the midst of things, it was hard to know which was which.

What had begun as a simple fact-minding mission for a client had become much more complicated, Bob reflected – and there was a lot that the boys still needed to find out if they were going to answer the questions on all of their minds. Who had killed Li Chang's father, and why? Had Li Chang's mother told the truth to the reporter who interviewed her after her husband was murdered? And was there really a stash of gold?

Bob needed to know the answers if he was going to write up his very first case online, and he was starting to worry that he might not get them. While it was true enough that the rock-bottom mysteries of life – particularly the mystery of what Worthington had called the in-tersection of human character and human in-telligence – could be fascinating in and of themselves, it was also true that mysteries de-manded resolutions, if they weren't to nag at you forever.

It had been a long and exciting day and it was time to put it behind him. Even so, as he climbed into his bunk, Bob found himself wondering if Angus O'Malley's letters would help The Three Investigators answer their unresolved questions about the mystery of Li Chang. He couldn't help but hope so!

10

Riding Shotgun

That night, Pete fell asleep quickly and dreamed of owls, gliding down from the trees, their eyes wide and yellow. When he awoke the next morning, for a moment he didn't know where he was. The ceiling was so close he could reach out and touch it, and when he did, he remembered all at once that he, Jupiter, Bob, and Worthington were in a cabin in the Gold Country. Appropriately enough, the light filtering in was warm and golden, and when Pete looked out the window, he could see that it was another cloudless day with a brilliant blue sky.

In the bunk beneath him, Bob was still asleep, and Jupe, in the metal-framed single, was hidden under a pile of sheets. What was that wonderful smell? Pete thought. It took little deduction to understand that Worthington had gotten up before them and was cooking break-fast. In one slick movement, Pete turned side-ways and slid from the bunk.

"Rise and shine!" he yelled as he landed on the floor.

Bob sat up, rubbing his eyes, but Jupiter just groaned and rolled over. "Come on," said Pete, "we have a big day ahead." He motioned to Bob, who grinned and quickly got up. Pete took the head and Bob the foot, and together they grabbed the metal-frame bed with Jupiter in it.

They were threatening to tip it sideways when Jupiter said, "All right, all right. I'm awake!"

Pete dressed quickly and joined Worthington in the cabin's main room. "Morning, Worthington," he said. "Gee! This is swell. Thanks a lot."

"Good morning, Pete," Worthington said. "I hope you're hungry."

"Hungry?" Pete said. "I'm starved!"

"That's a surprise," Jupiter said.

The four of them took their time over breakfast, and while the boys cleaned up, Worthington grabbed a cup of coffee and a tourist booklet he'd found out onto the porch. Pete was at the front of the line to the bathroom, and after he'd brushed his teeth and washed his face, he went outside to join Worthington on the porch. The two were sitting in friendly silence − Worthington reading and Pete watching a hawk high in the sky, riding the thermals

– when a car pulled into the campground and parked near the office.

The man who got out was Asian, and formally dressed. The day was heating up fast, but he wore a gray suit, well-shined shoes, and a bow tie. To Pete, he didn't seem the type to frequent a rough-and-ready campground like this one. Pete's curiosity had alerted Worthington, who put down the booklet and looked in the same direction Pete was looking.

In no time, the man had left the office and was striding toward the boys' cabin with a confident friendly air. Before he'd even reached the porch, he had his hand out for a handshake.

"You must be one of The Three Investigators," he said. He smiled as he looked at Pete. "Are you Jupiter Jones?"

Pete rose to his feet – as did Worthington – and Pete shook the man's hand.

"Golly," he said. "No, I'm Pete Crenshaw. Jupiter's in the cabin." He felt a bit flustered and didn't know what else to say.

"My name is John Chang," the man said. "I spoke by phone to you and your colleagues several days ago. Jupiter told me you'd be staying here when you arrived."

At the sound of a strange voice on the

porch, Jupiter and Bob came out of the cabin and stood next to Pete.

"Jupe, Bob," Pete said. "This is Mr. John Chang. Mr. Chang, this is Jupiter Jones and Bob Andrews, the other members of The Three Investigators. And this is our friend Worthington."

"Ah, yes," the man said. "The chauffeur."

Worthington shook the man's hand with a considerable lack of enthusiasm.

But John Chang's cheerfulness was relentless.

"I'm delighted to make your acquaintance," he said to Jupiter. "I've been reading what newspaper articles I could find online about you. I'm very impressed with your little enterprise; it seems you've never failed to solve a mystery that came to your attention."

"We're just three normal teenagers," Jupiter said. "But we've had a lot of luck."

Pete looked at Jupiter suspiciously. Jupe never used phrases like "normal teenagers" and he never attributed *anything* to luck.

At a glance Pete could tell that his friend had transformed himself into a dullard. He was pretending to be a lot less smart than he was as a way of lulling John Chang into a false sense of security. Jupiter had an uncanny ability to do this when he didn't like or trust the person he was speaking to. His face had gone a little slack, and his eyes, which usually sparkled with interest and intelligence, seemed heavy-lidded and incurious.

Worthington cleared his throat and looked meaningfully at Jupiter.

"I think I'll take a walk down by the creek, Master Jones," he said. "Just call me if you need me."

"Thank you, Worthington," Jupiter said.

"And you, young man," John Chang said. "You're Bob Andrews? Why, you look as if you're part Asian."

"My mother's parents were born in China, but I'm an American, just like you," Bob said. It seemed Bob didn't like John Chang much either, Pete thought.

With that, he remembered his manners. "Would you like a cup of coffee, Mr. Chang?" he asked. "Or tea?"

"No, thank you," Mr. Chang said as he took the chair Worthington had vacated. "I can't stay very long, I'm afraid. Much business to attend to back in Auburn. But I did want to welcome you to the area. I hope you're enjoying our neck of the woods. Have you discovered anything?"

"Not much," Jupiter said vacuously. "I'm afraid you were right about us coming up here in the first place."

Mr. Chang looked pleased. "Don't say I didn't warn you," he said. "It's a long way to come and not much to discover, I'm afraid. As I told you, there's no gold – an old rumor, nothing more, and long ago debunked. People so love the idea of buried treasure, don't they?" He smiled widely. Pete couldn't help notice how white his teeth were.

"Several of our cases have dealt with buried treasure," Bob said, "or if not buried exactly, then hidden – sometimes in plain sight."

"Yes," Mr. Chang said. "So I understand." His eyes glittered. "But I doubt any of the treasure you've uncovered had a curse upon it."

In that, he was wrong, Pete thought. The Indian jewel called the Fiery Eye had had a curse on it for a while. Luckily, that curse had also expired.

"Was there a curse on the gold?" Bob asked, following Jupiter's lead. "What kind of a curse?"

"A bad one," said John Chang.

"As we told you," Jupiter said. "We're doing historical research. That's all."

"Then perhaps I can help," John Chang said. "I'm hosting a meeting of the Gold Country Historical Society tonight at my home in Auburn. Perhaps the three of you would like to come? You might find it entertaining. Also, the house I live in is an Auburn landmark. It was built in the 1880s by a retired ship's captain who built in any number of ship's cupboards and a butler's pantry, and the like. I've only owned it for a year, but I've restored it in true Victorian colors and made sure that all the built-ins work properly again."

"That sounds interesting," Jupiter said, and for a moment his eyes gleamed. "We'd love to come."

"I'll see you this evening, then, around 7:00," John Chang said. He stood and shook the boys' hands and gave them his address. With a bright smile he turned and strode to his car. A minute later he was gone.

"You really don't trust that guy," Pete observed.

"Not even slightly," Jupiter said. "Everything about him makes me suspicious. Why would he bother to drive out here to welcome us? Why would he bring up the gold again only to tell us there isn't any, and then tell us about the curse? He was just trying to find out if we'd discovered anything. Also, when he called us in Yosemite, he told us he'd been hoping to get the money to conserve the one-room schoolhouse, but that the man who owned it had had to hire a demolition company to get rid of the rest of the structure after some hooligans had trashed it.

"But Gordon Small told us that John Chang himself was the land's owner. If so, he demolished the building himself. Bob, can we get online and see if we can find out anything more about John Chang?"

There was no Wi-Fi in the cabin, so Bob went to get his laptop and the boys took it to the campground's office and asked Randy if they could get online there. When he agreed, and gave them the campground's password, Bob loaded the genealogical website he had used to do the research on Li Chang. The free trial period hadn't yet ended and Pete watched as Bob researched the history of John Chang's family. The pages flew by more quickly than Pete could follow; one link led to another and Bob followed the trail like a bloodhound on a fresh scent.

"I thought so!" Bob said. As it turned

out, John Chang was a direct descendent of the man named Hao Chang – the much younger brother of Li Chang's father.

"It's a little odd that John Chang didn't mention he was descended from Li Chang's uncle," Jupiter said. "Let's see what we can find out about him."

Within minutes Bob's browser was filled with articles about John Chang – his son off to Stanford, his work with the historical society, his development plans for the vicinity around Auburn. Also, an article which seemed to imply that he was in financial trouble after a recent real estate venture that had failed badly.

"Wow!" said Pete. "What if he's trying to find the gold himself? What if he's trying to scare us off because of *that*?"

"An intelligent deduction," Jupiter said. "Whether or not there *is* gold, John Chang may be convinced there is."

He took a deep breath and looked at his watch. "Bob, can you check the times for the museum while you have your computer up? I want to get there as soon as it opens to examine Li Chang's graduation prize."

But when Bob pulled up the museum's website, it turned out it was closed for the day.

"Well," Jupiter said, "if that's the case,

we'll have to wait until tomorrow. Since we're not due at Connor O'Malley's house until noon, why don't we use the time between now and then to take a look at the place where the one-room schoolhouse was? Unless there's a No Trespassing sign on the land, there's no reason we can't walk on it, even if it *does* belong to John Chang."

When they asked Randy where it was, he said the place had no street address – which meant that they couldn't program anything into their GPS. Still, he gave them directions – which included a tree that had been hit by lightning, a falling-down barn, a creek, a clearing, and a hill. Pete was once again riding shotgun, and after Worthington managed to get them to the raw dirt road which marked the turnoff to the clearing Randy had described, he said to Pete, "It's up to you now." Pete leaned forward in his seat and started looking for the landmarks Randy had described.

Randy had told them that a four-wheel drive could get to the clearing where the schoolhouse had once stood, but the Land Rover soon left the road for what could only be called a trace – a few ruts and the suggestion of a path through tall dried grasses.

"Hang on," Worthington told the boys.

"Make sure you're buckled in."

"Wow!" Pete yelled. "We're off-roading."

"Yes, indeed," Worthington said. "Off-off roading."

Pete was the first to spot the live oak struck by lightning. Its center had been blasted and it looked like it was raising two fat green arms to the sky. The uneven rutted track began to level out. They soon came to the falling-down barn, where Worthington turned left and carved a path through the grass. The Land Rover dipped and came up the other side of a hollow and for a moment they were airborne. And then ahead of them was the creek.

Water splashed high on either side. They climbed the far bank, broke through a grove of trees, and were suddenly in a field that had recently been mowed. Ahead of them they could see a stone foundation.

"This must be it!" Pete said.

The four of them got out and surveyed the place. Though the foundation was broken and missing in spots, Pete could see that the building had been about twenty feet wide and thirty or thirty-five feet long. Most of the lumber had been carted away but the field still held scattered foundation stones, bits of wood, and a careful pile of lumber that looked as though it was waiting to be picked up.

Something caught Pete's eye and he dropped to his knees in the powdery dirt by the foundation. He scrabbled with his fingers, pulled out a piece of paper that he stuck in his pocket, and then picked up a little piece of something that glinted in the light.

"Hey! Look at this!" he cried. The others crowded around.

"What is it?" Bob asked.

It was encrusted with dirt, which Pete wiped away with his thumb.

"It's a pen nib," Jupiter said. "Like the ones we saw at the museum. The students had to keep dipping their pens in the ink to keep them from running dry. Maybe we can give it to Isabella Chang when we see her again, as a memento of this case." All four of them were staring down at the nib in Jupiter's palm when a shotgun blast went off behind them.

The boys yelled in surprise as a harsh voice said, "Turn around very slowly with your hands up." Pete raised his hands and turned. As he did, he thought of the rabbit's foot in his pocket and hoped it would help.

The woman was in her fifties or sixties, Pete thought, and she was pointing the shotgun she had already fired square at them. She was wearing an untucked canvas shirt and a long thin cotton skirt that went almost to the ground. Her eyes glittered with anger or madness or both. Her very long hair, strands of which fell over her shoulders and down her chest, was black and streaked with gray. Pete had never seen anyone like her before and was sorry to be seeing her now.

Worthington stepped forward.

"Madam," he said. "I must protest. These boys are under my protection."

She glared at him. "This is private property," she said. "No trespassing."

"We came to see the schoolhouse," Jupiter said.

"Well, it's not here any more." She motioned with the barrel of the shotgun toward the Land Rover. "Now go back where you came from. And don't let me see your faces again."

"Boys," Worthington said. "I suggest we do what the woman says."

She followed them, waving the gun, and pointed to a tree on the other side of the field.

"That way," she said.

The boys piled into the Land Rover as Worthington put the car into gear and eased away from the site of the old schoolhouse.

"Holy moly!" Pete said. "Annie Oakley! And *she's* the one who was riding shotgun!"

"I'm afraid so," Jupiter said.

Although Pete didn't want to show it, he was shaken. It was one thing to read about shotguns − or have Jupiter tell you stories about them − and another to have one pointed in your face by a woman wearing an untucked canvas shirt. John Chang had called her a prospector, but she'd seemed more like a lunatic to Pete.

They crossed the field and passed the tree. Fifty feet further on there was an old dirt road at the near end of which was a huge piece of plywood bolted to two posts sunk in the ground. As they passed, Pete turned to see that someone had spray-painted in large red letters the words NO TRESPASSING. Just a little further on they came to the main highway.

"We sure took the hard way," Bob said. "And we really didn't learn anything."

At that, Pete remembered the piece of paper he had thrust into his pocket. It was crumpled and dirty and a little torn, but when he dug it out and looked at it, he saw that it was the printout of an e-mail addressed to the manager of a company called Quinn Demolition & Salvage, and signed with the initials J.C.

It wasn't hard to figure out who J.C. was, because the sender's address was John Chang Construction.

The e-mail read: "Our agreement requires you to call me before you drive to the schoolhouse. I plan to watch the demolition, in case something of value turns up." On the bottom was written, in pencil, "Be sure to do what the client says. J. Quinn."

Wordlessly, Pete handed the paper to Jupiter.

Jupiter smiled a little grimly as he read. "This would seem to confirm that while John Chang was painting his big Victorian house in authentic Victorian colors, and making sure that all the built-ins work properly again, he was also overseeing the final destruction of Angus O'Malley's one-room schoolhouse. He was probably the one who tore it apart to begin with – almost certainly looking for Li Chang's gold."

"Where did that woman come from, anyway?" asked Pete.

Worthington nodded thoughtfully. "In the pamphlet I was reading this morning, it said that the area still has people living off the grid and panning for gold. A lot of them are squatters, but even though they have no legal right to the land they live on, they protect it as if they did. The creek we drove through could still be being panned."

"Maybe Connor O'Malley will be able to shed some light on that part of the conundrum," Jupiter said.

When Worthington pulled the Land Rover up the driveway of the address on Russell Road that Connor O'Malley had given them, Pete was surprised at how wild the place looked. Granted, given what Connor looked like, Pete hadn't expected a trim green lawn.

Still, the thick swords of century plants, the tangled brush, the live oaks, and the tall spindly grasses suggested that not much had been done with the property in some time. But the house itself, set back from the road, was tidy, brown-shingled, and weathered, with an overhanging porch on which Connor himself sat in a rocking chair, drinking a cup of coffee.

He rose and came down to the Rover, crying, "Welcome, welcome. Would you like to come in, too?" he said to Worthington. "I've made some lunch."

"That would be splendid," said Worthington, climbing out of the car.

Pete was glad to see the man who'd offered him such an adventure yesterday. He asked if Connor had gone back out to the soccer fields to check on their rescued friend, and Connor told him there was no sign of the great horned owl.

"He's fine, Pete," Connor said. "Thanks to you. About now I'll bet he's resting from a good night's hunting."

The downstairs was one big room, sparsely furnished and neat, with a few threadbare chairs arranged before a stone fireplace, a small kitchen in back, and a table with two chairs for eating. It was clear that Connor lived alone.

Except for the animals. Three cats lay curled on the chairs and a pair of finches sat on a perch in a large cage hanging from the ceiling. Buster, a very handsome and exceedingly friendly Boxer-Shepherd cross, greeted the boys in turn by jumping up, putting his paws on their chests, and licking their faces.

Though Jupiter seemed a bit uncertain how to react, Pete laughed with pleasure. "Good boy!" he said.

"I hope you're hungry," Connor said. He had put together a big fruit salad – strawberries and grapes, cantaloupe and watermelon – and they ate it with goat's milk yogurt that Connor had made. He had two goats in a pen in the back, and he told the boys he'd introduce them later.

When everyone had finished and pushed away their bowls, Connor asked the boys what, if anything, had happened since he'd seen them last.

"We went to the site of the schoolhouse where your great-great-grandfather taught," Pete said, "and some crazy woman with a shotgun fired a shot in the air and then told us to turn around with our hands up!"

When Connor looked astounded, Jupiter said, "Do you know who she was, or what she was doing there? Could she have been a squatter, panning for gold?"

"I guess she could have been," Connor said. "But firing her shotgun seems a pretty reckless thing to do."

"We also found this e-mail in the ruins of the schoolhouse," Jupiter said, handing it to Connor. "What do you think John Chang was hoping to find during the demolition?"

"John Chang," Connor said, "is a devious man. He's managed to fool a lot of people in Auburn and the surrounding area, but he hasn't managed to fool me. He's been tearing down old buildings, buying up property, and trying to build more and more houses in places where no houses should be built. There's too little water and the threat of fire is too great."

"But people keep coming to California," Pete said, "and they need somewhere to live."

"Fair enough," Connor said, "but everything needs to be balanced and carefully thought through. The Auburn Fire Department was able to put out the fire near the American River very quickly, but if it had spread up the canyon, the whole area could have been devastated – including the area where John Chang lives!"

"He's invited us to a meeting of the Gold Country Historical Society tonight, but I haven't looked to see how we get there," Bob responded.

"His house is on Aeolia Drive, above a grove of olive trees," Connor said. "It's a great house – just the kind that *should* be preserved, ironically enough. There's a lot of history in these old houses, and some families have lived in the area a long time."

"You told us yesterday that you still had all the letters you'd inherited," Jupiter said.

"Indeed," Connor said. "Going all the way back to the 1850s and filed by decade. Except if there were really a lot of them written by one person. Then they have their own folder.

But as I told you, I haven't read any of them."

"That's what I'm for," Bob said. "Records and Research."

"Except today we'll all be doing Bob's job," Pete said.

Connor smiled. "There's a small study upstairs – Buster, get down! – where I keep all my papers so I never have to look at them. You'll find that my house is more orderly than my studio. Up the stairs, turn right, second door on your left. I'll stay here and talk with Worthington."

"Thanks, Connor," Jupiter said. "We'll be careful."

"I know you will," Connor said. "I know the trustworthy sort when I see them."

Pete led the way up the stairs, and the boys found that the study was a small narrow room with a card table, a folding chair, and built-in bookshelves on one wall. There were books and piles of paper on most of the shelves, but on the bottom two shelves were neat document boxes made of heavy stock with labels on their spines.

Bob sat on the floor and started reading the labels.

"Letters – Mother, Dad, Uncle Seamus, Uncle Liam," he read. "Wow! Letters 1839-

1850. There are some old letters here.”

“Thank goodness Connor saved them,” Pete said. “Even if he didn’t read them.”

“Letters 1850-1860,” Bob read. And then his voice rose with excitement. “Guys! Here it is. Letters to Angus O’Malley.”

He pulled the box from the shelving and stood up. “Stand back,” he said. “Make way.” Pete beat his hands on the edge of the card table to imitate a drum roll, and as Bob flipped the top of the document box he added, “Ta da!”

And then he stood there, gazing incredulously.

The document box in Bob’s hands was empty. Completely empty. There were no letters in it at all.

11

A Perfect Plan

As Pete and Bob both said, "Oh no!", Jupiter stared into the box Bob held, feeling elated rather than dismayed. If Connor had stored Angus O'Malley's letters in this box, and if it was now empty, clearly someone had stolen the letters − and, although Jupiter could not be absolutely positive who had done that, the most obvious suspect was John Chang. Until that moment, he hadn't been certain if his deductions about the stash of gold were correct, or if his mistrust of John Chang was warranted. Now he felt justified on both counts.

When Pete saw Jupiter's face, he turned to him, astonished.

"Why are you so happy?" he asked.

"Because this event comes close to confirming our prior hypotheses," he said. "If John Chang is the one who stole the letters, then it seems highly probable that the woman with the shotgun wasn't as crazy as she looked − that she was actually hired by Chang to keep people away from the one-room schoolhouse while he tore it apart to see whether there was gold in it somewhere. Could you go down and ask Worthington and Connor to come up?"

Pete rushed away, down the stairs, and when he returned with the men behind him, Jupiter said to Connor, "I'm sorry to report that the letters appear to have been stolen. Have you noticed a break-in? Anything unusual or out of place?"

Connor stared at him, alarmed. "No," he said. "I never lock the house. It's so far back from the road. And I haven't noticed anything missing. When could this have happened?"

"When did you last see the letters?" Jupiter asked.

"It was months ago now. Three months, maybe. Something like that. I went through all these boxes, selected envelopes to use for my paintings, then copied them on my color printer. After I made the copies, I brought the letters back upstairs and put them back in their proper places. The letters to Angus O'Malley were bundled with rubber bands; there were three packets total, I think."

"Whoever took those letters could also have copied them − and then returned them. But he didn't," Jupiter said.

"Perhaps," said Worthington, "the thief didn't want to risk coming into the house twice."

"That makes sense," Connor said. "I don't keep regular hours, and whoever took them had no way of knowing when I might be here."

"Or," Bob said, "the person who took them thought keeping the originals was worth the risk."

"I have a pretty good idea who that person is," Jupiter said. "From the beginning I've been curious about how insistent John Chang was that no stash of gold had ever existed. He tried hard to keep us from coming up here."

"Yeah," Pete said, "and this morning he was trying to scare us with that talk of a curse."

"This is making more and more sense," Connor said. "The Gold Country Historical Society has been asked to make an assessment of the old Carnegie Library, and John Chang came around about two months ago to see what we artists were up to. He walked around the studios, his hands behind his back like an overseer – careful not to get paint on his fancy clothes. When he took a good look at the canvases I was working on, he suddenly became quite animated and started asking about them. I told him just what I told you. That I'd taken the letters out of the envelopes and saved them."

"And just like us," Jupiter said, "he must have seen the painting of the envelope addressed to Angus O'Malley."

"Jeez!" Pete said. "This is getting complicated."

"But it's making more and more sense," Connor said. "I get the feeling that John Chang is stretched pretty thin these days. I'd say he might even be headed for bankruptcy. When he bought that place on Aeolia Drive, I don't think he actually could afford it."

"So a hidden stash of gold would come in pretty handy," Pete said.

As Pete and Bob talked eagerly with Connor and Worthington, Jupiter stood looking out the window, thinking. If Chang had learned about the letters to Angus O'Malley about the same time he knew he might be heading toward bankruptcy, he had probably stolen the letters from Connor just in case they held a clue to the rumored gold. From Chang's obsessive interest in The Three Investigators, Jupiter thought it likely that, even if they *did* hold a clue, they hadn't helped Chang know where the gold was actually hidden.

Jupiter theorized that once John Chang

had become convinced the gold was hidden *somewhere*, he had started to tear apart the schoolhouse and had also hired the woman with the shotgun to scare people away from the site. However, even when he had the schoolhouse completely torn apart, he was no further along than he'd been when he'd started. Everything was coming together, and Jupiter had that pleasant buzzing behind the eyes he felt when the end of a mystery was in sight.

"Connor," Jupiter said. "As Bob mentioned, John Chang has invited us to his house tonight for a meeting of the Historical Society. Do you know anything particular about his house?"

"Only that it's a grand old Victorian, high on a hill on Aeolia Drive, overlooking the American River canyon," Connor said. "He bought it through Ambrosia Realty about a year ago. Beautiful place, and historic. Extensive grounds. Palm trees on either side of the entrance."

"But you've never been inside it?"

"John Chang wouldn't invite me to his house any more quickly than I'd invite him to mine," Connor said.

"But remember," Pete said. "He broke into yours."

"If my hunch is right," Jupiter said, "Chang will have kept the letters rather than destroying them, in case they hold a code or secret message – something he hasn't figured out yet. I think we should try to find them while we're visiting him tonight – and if we *do* find them, steal them back."

"Steal them?" Pete said in alarm.

"Really, we'll simply be returning them to their rightful owner," Jupiter explained.

"Turnabout is fair play, if I may say so," Worthington said.

Jupiter paced the room, pinching his lip. "This is a difficult conundrum," he said. "We've been invited to a meeting, so the house will have any number of strangers in it. How do we search the house without being apprehended?"

"I have an idea," Bob said. "We need to try to figure out where the letters might be hidden before we get there. If Chang bought the house only a year ago, maybe the real estate company that sold it still has the listing on line. I'll get my laptop and see if we can find pictures of the interior."

"An excellent suggestion," said Jupiter.

The five of them trooped down the stairs. Bob grabbed his laptop, and, with Connor's help, got on his Wi-Fi network. In no time he was on the website of Ambrosia Realty. Its owner, Ambrosia DiSalvio, had extensive listings, as well as a backlog of all the properties she'd sold in the last two years. Bob quickly found a listing for a Victorian house on Aeolia Drive, and when Bob pulled up the photos, Connor nodded his head.

"Wow!" Pete said. "Look at that purchase price."

"It probably stretched Chang to the limit," Connor said. "He was gambling that it would be a showcase to further enhance his reputation. He didn't foresee the trouble that lay ahead for his business interests."

"This is a mansion!" Pete said as Bob scrolled through the pictures of the interior. The house had fourteen rooms including two sitting rooms with marble fireplaces, a formal dining room to seat twenty, a solarium, a library, a study, five bedrooms, a "games" room with a pool table, a wine cellar, and an in-ground pool.

Jupiter studied the photos carefully, looking for places where Chang might have hidden the letters, but nothing jumped out at him. Maybe there were sliding panels or revolving shelves. Maybe there was a hidden safe behind a painting. This was going to be more difficult than he'd imagined.

"Whoa," Pete said. "Get a load of this." He pointed to a block of text right under the address.

Jupiter had been looking at the pictures and had neglected to read the description of the estate, written by the realtor. "One-of-a-kind," he read. "Stunning 1880s Victorian on the market for the first time in over fifty years."

The text went on to detail the view, the rooms, the wine cellar, the pool. "Wonderfully eccentric built-ins," it concluded. "Mahogany bookshelves, marble fireplace mantels, secret windowsill drawer."

"Secret windowsill drawer!" Pete said. "What do you think?"

Jupiter said, "I think John Chang is just the kind of man who would hide the letters in such a drawer. But how will we discover which windowsill the drawer is under? I wonder if we could deduce it from looking closely at the pictures. Perhaps there is something about the windowsill which will make it stand out from the others."

There was also a floor plan on the realty site, and Jupiter asked Connor for permission to print it out and take it with him. He then studied the pictures again. They had been taken very carefully. Each room had at least three exposures, and after looking at all the rooms on the ground floor, Jupiter was almost certain that the only window that looked significantly different from the others was on the side of the room that also held the bookshelves, and was labeled as a study.

That window had what seemed a slightly wider sill, and also an apron underneath it that had a curious double notch on either side. If you weren't already looking for a secret windowsill drawer, you would never notice the difference from the other windows in the house, but if you were, the difference seemed apparent.

When he showed the others, they agreed.

"That has to be it!" Pete said.

Still, Jupiter thought, it was one thing to know where to look and another to be able to do so. The boys thanked Connor for his help and told him that if they found the letters that night at John Chang's house, they'd bring them back to him at once – at least if he was going to be there.

He said he was, and when they'd said goodbye, Worthington drove them back to their cabin. All the way there, Jupiter kept pinching his lower lip.

"Careful," Pete said at one point. "You'll hurt yourself."

Jupiter smiled thinly. He needed to figure out a way to get Chang and the other members of the Historical Society out of the house so that he could search the study unimpeded. But how to do that?

And then it came to him. Although everyone in California was always at least a *little* frightened of fire, he would bet that anyone who lived above the American River canyon and had seen the smoke from the campsite fire the day before would be particularly jangled at the thought that the fire department might have missed something. If he could get Chang and his other guests to believe there was a fire in the canyon below the house, that would surely get them outside.

When he and Bob and Pete had been talking firebugs, back in Rocky Beach, and Pete had said that lightning strikes and high-voltage utility lines were bad enough without people running around starting fires, Bob had observed – quite rightly – that everyone was so on edge these days that it would be easy to fool someone into leaving their house unlocked and

215

unprotected by just knocking on their door, pointing into the distance, and yelling 'Fire!'

Jupiter himself had noted that people were amazingly easy to frighten – that they rarely required solid evidence to back up assertions if their own safety was involved. Little had he known, at the time, that this observation might prove the key to solving The Three Investigators' first mystery of the summer!

All the way back to the cabin, and for the rest of the afternoon, Jupiter perfected the plan with the help of Bob and Pete and Worthington. After they'd been at John Chang's house for twenty minutes or so, Worthington – who would stay outside with the Land Rover – would ring the bell and say that, although he wasn't certain, he thought he saw smoke in the canyon.

Chang would undoubtedly want to look for himself, and his guests would follow. Pete and Bob would talk excitedly to Chang, keeping him occupied and outside, and – with the help of the floor plan – Jupiter would find the secret windowsill drawer and remove what he hoped would be three packets of envelopes containing letters. Those packets might be a little bulky, and since he really couldn't just stick them in the pocket of his pants, he needed to find a way to conceal them on his body.

Luckily, Bob had brought with him on the trip a zippered pouch – like an extra-large Zip-loc bag, but black and sturdy and with an actual zipper – to keep his notes in. The pouch was really for camping and had four Velcro straps sewn to its edges so that it could be fastened on the outside of a pack, if necessary. Those Velcro straps would also work to fasten the pouch around Jupiter's middle.

With the zip left open and the pouch strapped to his chest, Jupiter should be able to quickly unbutton his shirt and slip the letters in, he thought. Soon after – when the hubbub about the fire had passed – Bob would complain of a stomach ache, and the three of them would make their apologies and get out of there.

It was a perfect plan, Jupiter thought. He tried not to think of what he would do if the letters weren't in the secret drawer, and soon enough, they were driving to John Chang's house. Though Aeolia Drive was close to downtown Auburn, it felt like a world apart. Jupiter marveled as Worthington drove the Land Rover slowly along the twisting narrow lane cut into the side of a steep hill.

To their right, an olive orchard – the

leaves of the olive trees silver in the waning light – fell sharply away toward the American River canyon, while to their left houses perched precariously, carved into the red dirt of the hillside. Some of the driveways were so steep Jupiter wondered how a car could even get up them. It was amazing what people would do for a view of the world. The farther they went, the larger the houses became. This was where the rich people lived.

Though Jupiter knew his plan was risky, when he saw the canyon for himself, he thought the part about the fire would simply *have* to work. All of California was on edge during the dry season, and the American River canyon was at very high risk for a wildfire.

Its steep walls were covered with dried grasses, manzanita, greasewood, coyote brush, and other shrubs, and the pitch of the land would make firefighting very difficult. If there ever were a fire in the canyon, it could sweep right up the hill, and this road was so twisty and narrow it would be difficult for people to escape. No pyromaniacs needed.

"Now, remember," Jupiter said to Worthington. "Don't wait more than twenty minutes before you sound the alarm."

"He knows, Jupe," Pete said. "You've

told him a zillion times."

"Sorry, Worthington," Jupiter said. "I guess I'm a little anxious."

"I quite understand," Worthington said.

"And when John Chang answers the door," Jupiter said, "make sure you don't say there's *definitely* a fire. Just tell him you think you saw smoke in the canyon. Play it down. We don't want you to get in any trouble."

"I won't be calling the fire department, Jupiter," Worthington said, smiling. "And please remember that I'm a professional actor." His voice had deepened and his English accent gotten more pronounced. Bob laughed.

"After all," Worthington added. "It could be haze. It could be a cloud. Chang's fear will do the rest."

"Perfect," Jupiter said. "I think that's it." He pointed. "Up on that hill."

The Victorian looked both odd and impressive as it caught the last rays of the sun. The shingled siding was a charcoal blue, the trim white, the ornamentation light yellow. The entrance to the property was off a side road and led to a small parking area already crowded with cars. The boys and Worthington got out, and Worthington smiled and tipped his imaginary cap.

"Good luck," he said. "Call me if you need me."

"Thanks, Worthington," Jupiter said. "I know we can count on you."

He took the lead and the three boys walked around the house on the brick walkway. Pete whistled; the house commanded an imposing view for miles across the canyon. They mounted the wooden steps to the tall double glass-fronted doors set back on the ornate porch. Jupiter rang the bell and John Chang answered it, his face wreathed in a smile, looking as fresh as he had that morning.

"Ah," he said. "My young friends."

He took them into a sitting room where he introduced them to the other members of the Historical Society – which included another Chinese man who stood next to John Chang, almost as if he was his bodyguard. He had jet-black hair and guarded eyes. On his cheek was a livid scar – the kind of scar that would only have come from a knife fight.

"Ladies and gentlemen," John Chang said grandly, "these are the boys I told you about. They call themselves The Three Investigators, and they're visiting us from southern California. I won't take the time to introduce everyone personally, but I hope you'll do that yourselves during our break. Boys, there are refreshments in the dining room, if you care for any."

Pete started to walk in that direction, but Jupiter caught his arm. He had put on his invisible disguise again as soon as they'd arrived and he made his voice as dull and lackluster as he could.

"No, thank you, Mr. Chang," he said. "Maybe later."

There were three empty chairs arranged as part of a circle, and Jupiter and his friends sat down. As he did, Jupiter looked around him to match what he was seeing with the floor plan he had memorized.

"We were talking," John Chang said, "about the desks from the schoolhouse my distant cousin attended – the one you boys know about – and the anti-Chinese graffiti we found under several of the lids. It's distressing that prejudice directed at our forebears is still with us today."

The members of the Society murmured agreement. Jupiter kept his face blank. Discrimination and prejudice were very bad things, of course, but sometimes, he thought, people took offense when none was intended – indeed, where none was to be found.

He continued to orient himself in accordance with his memory of the floor plan. There was the sitting room he was in, with the dining room behind. If he went back out to the foyer and then down the hall, the study he was seeking would be the third door on the right.

John Chang had begun talking about the obstacles he'd faced because of his ancestry. Jupiter looked at Bob and Pete. Pete fidgeted in his chair, looking uncomfortable. Bob seemed more angry than uncomfortable.

"Excuse me, Mr. Chang," he said. "It's only my opinion, but my mother is Chinese-American, and though she's faced some obstacles, it seems that people like her are doing pretty well these days. And pardon me for saying so, but it looks like you've done pretty well, too."

"Well, yes," John Chang said. "But – "

Bob kept on talking. "The hatred of the Chinese in the 19th century was awful," he said. "No doubt about it. But things are much, much better today, don't you agree?"

John Chang looked as if he was about to agree, but Bob didn't give him time.

"Why would anyone want to think of himself as a victim when he could think of himself as a winner, instead?" he asked. "Besides,

I've heard stories about what things were like in in the late 1960s in China itself – when my mother's parents barely got out with their lives. Even today the Chinese Communist Party treats the Chinese people with an oppressive hand."

Jupiter was impressed at the clarity with which Bob made his comments, but John Chang's smile was strained.

"Apples and oranges, my young friend," he said.

But he quickly changed the subject and began talking about the Society's plan to erect a marker at the site of the old Placer County Hospital cemetery in memory of all the people once buried there.

Just then the doorbell rang.

"Who can this be?" John Chang said. "I wasn't expecting anyone else." He got up and strode to the door.

Everyone in the sitting room sat quietly, smiling politely. The murmurs in the foyer grew louder, and Jupiter could hear the change in John Chang's tone. The man came hurriedly back into the room, looking both very serious and a little frightened.

"I'm afraid," he said, "I've just been told there may be another fire in the canyon. Near where the fire was put out yesterday, I think."

Everyone stood up at once, and the expressions of alarm were universal. Jupiter felt a little badly about having given all these people a shock, but he was glad the plan was working. John Chang turned and started outside to the front lawn, followed by his guests.

"Go get 'em," Pete said to Jupiter.

"You bet," said Jupiter. "Now be sure to talk John Chang's ear off. The longer you can keep him outside, the better. The others will stay wherever he is."

Pete and Bob followed Chang and his guests outside while Jupiter went in the opposite direction. Third door on the right, and he was in the study. His heart was hammering in his chest; he was so close to getting what he'd come for, but also so close to getting caught.

One wall of the study was floor-to-ceiling bookcases crowded with books. There was a desk not far from the window Jupiter had identified on the realty site, with a number of manila folders neatly arranged on a blotter on its top. Jupiter glanced behind him at the door, then glanced at the folders very quickly. They seemed to be mainly financial records, but one of them was marked Auburn Carnegie Library, and Jupiter wished he had time to investigate it further.

Since he didn't, he hurried to the window, got to his knees, put his fingers in the double notches on either side, and pulled. The apron began moving soundlessly outward, toward him. The letters were there! Three thick packets, fastened with green rubber bands. He unbuttoned his shirt, slid the letters into the pouch that had been taped to his chest, then buttoned his shirt carefully up again. He was just getting to the front door, planning to join the others, when John Chang appeared, closely followed by Pete and Bob.

Chang looked at him suspiciously.

"I was just using the bathroom," Jupiter said. "Is everything O.K.?"

"It seems to have been a false alarm," Chang said.

Still, everyone was jittery and talking at once. Chang suggested that refreshments were in order — which was when Bob said that all the tumult had made him dizzy and he was feeling a little sick.

"Oh, no," Jupiter said. "Not again."

They apologized heartily for having to leave early, and though Jupiter knew Pete was following the script, he kept casting rueful glances in the direction of the finger sandwiches and trays of cookies. But they were soon out the door and back in the Land Rover.

As Worthington pulled out of the property and back onto Aeolia Drive, he said, "An excellent plan, Jupiter. It went off without a hitch, just as you said it would. And were you equally successful?"

Jupiter unbuttoned his shirt and unzipped the document pouch. He pulled out the letters and brandished them. "Gentlemen," he said. "Angus O'Malley's missing correspondence."

12

Free To All

Bob's excitement mounted as he stared at the envelopes in Jupiter's hand. When The Three Investigators used logic and reasoning to solve a puzzle, he was always thrilled. Besides, now that Jupiter had found the stolen letters, there was every reason to think they were closing in on the end of the story.

Although Connor had only used four of the Angus O'Malley letters in his envelope paintings – and those hadn't had return addresses with names on them – Bob could see that Jupiter was holding three thick packets. Bob was itching to get his hands on them, and Pete, in the front seat next to Worthington, was so fired up he looked like he might try to jump into the back.

"Let's all stay calm," Jupiter said. "We've got the letters now and they're not going anywhere. It won't be long until we're back at Connor's house. We'll read them there."

"I can't stay calm," Pete said. "I think I'm going to pop. Do you think one of them will say where the gold is?"

"I'm afraid the letters won't tell us that on their own," Jupiter said. "If they did, John Chang would already have his hands on it."

"They were really in the secret drawer under the window?" Bob asked.

"They were," said Jupiter. "A very clever hiding place, and one I thought John Chang would find difficult to resist."

At the end of Aeolia Drive, Worthington turned right on Lincoln Way, and a few miles later he turned again onto Russell Road. The sun had now set and the shadows were long. As they drove up Connor's driveway, the Land Rover's headlights caught a rabbit sitting calmly, its pink eyes staring, before it hopped off into the darkness.

Worthington pulled up in front of the porch and parked, and as he and the boys got out, Connor came to the door.

So did Buster, who pushed open the screen and launched himself at Pete.

"Buster!" Pete said. He hunkered down beside the dog, who licked his face, then flopped onto his back for a belly rub.

"As good as your word," Connor said. "What have you got?"

"The letters!" Bob said. "We found them. Or rather Jupiter did."

"We all did," Jupiter said. "I couldn't have done it alone."

"Come in, come in," Connor said. "Let's see what they say. If I'd read them before, I could have saved you all a lot of trouble."

He invited them in to the living room after shooing various sleeping cats from the chairs.

"So lazy!" Connor said, shaking his head. "Can't be bothered to do anything other than sleep or eat." He'd turned on a number of lights and a warm glow suffused the room. Buster lay at his feet, panting happily.

"Bob," Jupiter said, "I think that you, as Records and Research, ought to be the one to read the letters."

He handed the packets of envelopes to Bob, who took off the rubber bands that had kept the envelopes together and shuffled through the stack. They were all addressed to Angus O'Malley, but since they had come from different authors, the look of Angus's address varied wildly from one to the next.

Mostly, the address had been written in black ink, sometimes more legibly than at others; some of Angus's correspondents had printed his name in oversized letters and others were written in an elegant script almost like calligraphy. Several had return addresses in Ireland. The stamps were colorful, and all of them had been postmarked by hand.

When Bob found one with the name Rose O'Malley Chang at the top of the return address – on the back flap of the envelope – his heart leapt.

"Here's a letter from Li Chang's mother," he said. "She was Angus O'Malley's cousin, remember. She and Angus came over from Ireland together."

Bob carefully removed the letter from the envelope and unfolded it. The page was covered with careful script, written with a fine nib and black ink. The letters were a bit faded in spots, which made it hard to read.

"She writes very well," Bob said. "Maybe she was educated at the same hedge school as Angus." He steadied his voice, which had risen in his excitement.

"The letter is dated 1875, two years after Li Chang graduated from Mr. O'Malley's school, if I've got my dates right."

Pete interrupted. "You've always got your dates right, Bob!"

"Thanks," Bob said. "Here's how it starts: '*My dear Angus, I write to you today to answer your many questions, though it causes me great pain to do so.'"*

Bob looked up at the faces of the others who were peering at him with intense interest. Pete was nodding feverishly, with a smile on his lips.

"Li and I are as well as could be hoped for, thanks be to God. The laundry has few customers as of yet, but that is to be expected; after all, we have just begun, and people are suspicious of newcomers. Li is still very upset at the loss of his father, as am I, of course, and the circumstances make it even worse.

"As you have guessed, I did not tell the whole truth to the reporter from the Auburn paper. I did not lie when I said that my husband was murdered by another Chinaman, but I was false in saying I did not know who the devil was."

"Wow!" Pete said.

Jupiter sat forward eagerly, his hands clasped together. Bob could see he, too, could barely contain his curiosity.

Bob scanned the letter and felt a wave of shock. He looked up at his friends in consternation.

"My gosh!" he said. "Li's father was killed by his own younger brother! Hao Chang. The man John Chang is descended from."

"Holy moly!" Pete said. "His own brother!"

Bob read the rest of the letter as his friends and the two men sat in rapt attention. The facts were these: Li's father had been panning for gold ever since he'd arrived in the mining camp and he'd filled a small leather pouch – he called it an *envelope* – with nuggets he'd found in the sand and grime at the bottom of the creek. The envelope was "small but very heavy," according to his widow. To everyone but her, he pretended he'd found nothing other than a few gold flakes, but a rumor had spread that he'd been more successful than he'd let on. He'd hidden the pouch under the floor of the small wooden shack where he lived with Rose and Li.

The evening of the murder, Hao Chang and another Chinese man had come to the mining camp and barged into the shack. At first they'd wheedled for a hand-out, with Hao reminding Li's father about the responsibility he had to his family. But Li's father had remained stony-faced and unmoved; he'd never liked this younger brother or thought he owed him anything. Then Hao threatened him and pressured him to reveal where he'd been panning. The three men were leaving camp on mules laden down with saddlebags when they started to argue.

Li's mother was watching from the kitchen window as Hao dismounted, came to the side of her husband's mule, and reached for his saddlebags. Her husband had kicked at Hao, catching him in the chest. The younger man sprawled in the dirt, and when he got back up, he held a pistol in his hand. The gun went off and Li's father toppled from the saddle. It had all happened very quickly.

"*I was sobbing and praying to God,*" Bob read. "*My husband lay in the dirt as the two fiends frantically searched the saddlebags. Of course they found nothing. The pistol shot had brought people out of their shacks and the murdering thieves rode off in a panic. I had to keep Li safe, and even though it seemed likely that Hao had shot my husband without planning to do so beforehand, I couldn't risk telling anyone who had done this deed. If he found out, Hao might kill me or my son. My son was just six months from graduating from your school, so I waited until he had his diploma to move with him to Auburn and start a new life here.*

"*The gold is safely hidden. I have told no one where it is. I fear I can never use it, though. I was ranting in rage and grief when I talked to the reporter, and in my upset, I put a fifty-year curse upon whatever gold my husband might have had. 'A widow's curse upon it,' I said. 'Six horse loads of graveyard clay upon it; may hell's seventeen devils go after it.*'"

"Well, that would do it," Pete said. "And

we're sure the curse has expired?”

“Yes,” Bob said. “Almost a hundred years ago. Here's how the letter ends.”

"*'I think my curses will keep the thieves from looking, but I am now afraid to spend any of the gold myself. Be that as it may, if it is indeed accursed gold, it will remain that way for fifty years. The old superstitions die hard, Angus, as you know, and even though Li pokes fun at me and tells me they are only silly words, I think it will be good for him to make his way in the world, as his father did. I will make him promise to keep the gold hidden and safe until the fifty years is up. It will then be up to him to decide whether to test the curse.'*"

“An amazing story,” Connor said. “Rose Chang was a strong and resourceful woman.”

“With a good head for business,” Bob said. “She made a great success of the laundry and dry goods store, and, as it turned out, didn't need the gold to help her.”

Jupiter said, "This is the first time we've gotten any real idea of the size or worth of Li's father's treasure. If he indeed had a small but heavy leather pouch filled with nuggets, we could be on the trail of a fortune. But so far, we still have no idea where the gold is hidden.”

"We're not done with the letters yet,” Bob said. He looked through the other envelopes carefully before pulling another one from the pack.

"This one's postmarked 1919," he said. "From Li Chang's widow. That's the year after the flu epidemic that killed him."

He took out the letter. The paper was very thin, a kind of onionskin, and the writing was careful, beautifully done.

He looked up at the other four. "It's a letter asking for help," he said. "If I've got my facts straight, Li's widow would have been in her early sixties, and writing to Angus the year after Li died – when Angus was close to 90. The address on the envelope is Sacramento, not Cool, so clearly Angus O'Malley had left the Auburn area some time before – maybe after he stopped teaching. It's possible Li had never even introduced his old teacher to his wife."

Bob read the letter through to its end, then told the others that though Li hadn't known where the gold was hidden in 1875 when he was just sixteen, his mother had obviously told him before she died. According to Li's widow, Li had hidden it himself some years earlier. She was writing to ask if Angus had any idea where it might be. Though the laundry was still holding its own, she wanted the money to send her grandson to college.

"And listen to this!" Bob said. "*'Master, when my honored husband was so sick with the fever, he was sometimes not in his right mind. The herbalist came each day and gave him White Tiger Decoction and hot ginger soup, but it did not help. He grasped my hand so hard I feared my fingers would break. He kept whispering 'Athena, goddess of wisdom' and 'Free to all.' Do you have any idea what he was trying to tell me? I know the book you gave him, and the words above the library, but what do they mean? Right before he closed his eyes for the last time, he said, 'The demons, the demons,' as if he were afraid that they were coming to snatch him. Can you help a poor widow? He had told me the gold was cursed by his mother, but I know he would have wanted his grandson and son and wife to have this money to help them in this world.'*"

"Angus O'Malley was very, very old," Worthington said. "Perhaps he was never able to write back to her."

"Even if he had," Jupiter said, "I don't know what he could have told her that she didn't already know about the book and the library."

"So that's why she put FREE TO ALL on Li Chang's gravestone," Bob said. "Along with the Owl of Athena. She was honoring his last words, even if she didn't understand them any more than *we* do."

Bob was moved by the piteous tone of the letter and wondered why Li had not told his wife more than he had. He looked at Jupiter, whose face had assumed an expression of intense repose. He was thinking hard.

"I hope this is making more sense to the four of you than it is to me," Connor said.

"Sorry, Connor," Bob said. He went over the story quickly, filling in whatever details Connor hadn't known so that he could stitch everything together into a coherent pattern.

"Well, I could use a cup of tea," Connor said. "Worthington?"

Worthington expressed great pleasure at the idea, though Bob and the others said they were too jittery with excitement.

While the tea was steeping, Connor took them out onto the back deck. He flicked a switch and two spotlights lit up a chicken coop, a few errant chickens who hadn't yet roosted for the night, a rooster who looked quite perturbed at the sudden brightness, and a pen with two white goats. Further back in the yard was a fire pit for campfires, and beyond that, an octagonal gazebo made of what looked like cedar or redwood, with a shingled roof.

Connor led the way, opening and closing

several gates, until the boys stood in the small pen with him and the goats.

"This is Daisy," Connor said. As if by magic he produced a slice of apple and she came running to him and ate out of his hand. "I didn't forget you, Mae," he said.

Bob liked the feeling of the goats pushing against him, their insistence and the warmth of their bony heads. Pete looked ecstatic.

"I really admire goats," Connor said. "They're friendly and curious; they'll eat just about anything, if they get the chance. You've got to be very careful with what they have access to.

"Daisy and Mae are Saanen goats, which is the most popular dairy breed. Each produces up to a gallon of milk a day, which keeps me plenty busy, I can tell you! I've had goats for years now. I'm even a sponsor for the Gold Country 4-H club – for boys and girls raising goats as a project."

Night had settled in, though Bob could still see streaks of tangerine and pink in the western sky.

Connor shooed the rest of the chickens back into the coop and secured them for the night. The rooster took up his position on the coop's roof and fixed Connor with a bright eye.

Back inside, Connor and Worthington drank tea, while Bob picked up the envelopes again and methodically went through them, taking every letter out of its envelope, skimming it quickly and then reinserting it. Several of the letters were from old students writing to thank Angus O'Malley for what he had given them, or to reminisce about the days when they'd been students in the one-room schoolhouse. As he read one such letter sent from a man who had moved to San Francisco, Bob was thrilled to discover what seemed a very solid clue.

"Listen to this!" he said to Pete and Jupe. "It's from one of Angus's students who went to school at the same time Li Chang did. It seems they both loved puzzles and were good at them. When they had a bit of extra paper, they would sometimes pass notes to one another during class. Their notes would just be lists of numbers, because they were using a book cipher."

"A book cipher!" Jupiter said. "We've run into those before."

"That's right," Pete said excitedly. "In the mystery with the screaming clock!"

Jupiter nodded. "An old, established way to send a secret code."

When Connor looked blank, Jupiter went

on: "If two people have the same edition of the same book, all they have to do is figure out what message they want to send, then look for the words of their message in the book. The code is a set of numbers, in pairs separated by a dash. Usually, the first number is the page of the book and the second number refers to the word. Five dash thirty-six means page 5, the 36th word."

Connor still looked a little blank, but Jupiter moved on, with suppressed excitement.

"Good work, Bob!" he said.

"Remember what Li Chang said to his wife when he was dying?" Bob said to Pete. "If he had left a coded message, what book do you suppose he used?"

"*Athena, Goddess of Wisdom,*" Pete yelled. Then he stopped and his excitement faded. "But we don't have any numbers!"

Bob had thought of that, too. However, he'd also remembered that the last time The Three Investigators had unraveled a book cipher, they'd thought they were at a dead end because half of the message was lost. But the creator of the cipher had done what a lot of people do when they're working on one – put a faint pencil line under the words he was using. If they were lucky, Li Chang had done the same thing.

He explained this to Pete and Worthington and Connor. Jupiter needed no explanation; his mind had jumped to the same possibility that Bob's had.

"We'll find out tomorrow when we get to the museum," he said. "If there's a message, it should take us to the gold."

"Now you're talking!" Pete said. "I knew it was there all along."

"Remember, of course," Jupiter said. "The treasure will belong to Isabella Chang."

Even so, Bob thought, they'd have the excitement of finding it and the pleasure of restoring it to its rightful owner – who was Li Chang's direct descendent. This had turned into a very satisfying case, after all, full of twists and turns. It had started small, but as one fact had led to another, it had gotten larger and more complex. And there were lots of clues – graduation plaques, Greek primers, paintings of envelopes and letters.

As with life itself, the challenge came in distinguishing between the false clues and the real ones, then putting them together in the right order.

"Well," Connor said, "I'm happy for you. But I guess this means that if you solve your case, you'll be leaving soon to go back to Rocky Beach. I was just getting used to having the four of you around."

"You can always come visit," Pete said. "And bring Buster."

Connor laughed. "Are you inviting me or my dog? By the way, how did the three of you meet?"

"We met when we started kindergarten in Rocky Beach, and since all of us were the only children in our families, we were drawn together from the start," Jupiter said.

"Also, our birthdays are in August, September, and October," Pete said. "Jupe's August, Bob's September, and I'm October," he added. "That means we're all on the young end of our school class."

For some reason, Bob thought of Mallory MacLeod when Pete said this. He didn't know how old she was, exactly, but he'd liked her a lot. He remembered the way she'd stared up at the talisman at the Salvage Yard, and the talk they'd had outside the library. With most girls, he couldn't quite relax, but with Mallory he'd found that, in no time at all, they had gotten beyond gossip and chitchat and were talking about real things. He thought with chagrin that, so far, she hadn't called him.

They said goodbye to Connor and climbed back in the Land Rover. By now, it was totally dark, and Worthington drove them to Cabin 5 at the Sighing Pines Campground more slowly than usual. When they got there, they were all still wide awake, and they sat on the porch talking about the day. At least, Jupiter and Pete talked. Bob was pretty silent, thinking about a great idea he'd come up with for future Three Investigators' cases.

Almost as soon as he'd heard Hector Sebastian use the phrase *Abecedarian Academy*, he'd decided that if The Three Investigators ended up finding out something interesting for Isabella Chang, he would file it as *The Mystery of the Abecedarian Academy*.

However, only when he'd been handling Connor O'Malley's letter files had it occurred to him that since a lot of documents were filed alphabetically, maybe he could actually file his case reports that way. If the first one had two As in it, maybe the second one could have two Bs.

After all, although Jupiter had had a great idea when he'd come up with three question marks as The Three Investigators' trademark (and "We Investigate Anything" as their motto) it couldn't hurt to remember what Hector Sebastian had said about the human mind liking to find patterns. He'd said that if you want to capture someone else's imagination, you have to give them a pattern that can be easily remembered. What could be better than the Roman alphabet? Bob thought. After all, everyone began their education with the alphabet. Everyone who lived in a country which *used* an alphabet, at least.

In any case, although Bob had been feeling anxious for a while about having the sole responsibility of writing up The Three Investigators cases, now that he'd started to imagine his future reports lined up on a shelf, so to speak – with a C title following the B one and a D title following the C – he thought he could rise to the task of writing them. For one thing, he liked keeping mental files even more than he liked keeping physical ones, and for another, he liked the idea of coming up with odd adjectives or weird combinations of adjectives and nouns.

As Bob sat on the porch, thinking about all this, Pete suddenly got to his feet and stretched.

"I didn't tell you this earlier," Bob said, "but Mallory MacLeod? She's spending the week at a Scottish music camp with her mother. In Grass Valley."

Pete whistled in surprise. "That town to the north of us?"

"Well," Bob said. "Somewhere around here."

"You know," Pete said. "Ever since the three of us started working together, I've thought it would be cool having a girl operative. Do you know where the camp is, Bob? Maybe we could see her."

"I think not," Jupiter said decisively. "One of the principles of investigation is staying on track. We can't let ourselves get diverted now, especially when we're so close."

Bob had to admit that Jupe was right. They had to keep their eye on the prize, not the girl.

13

Stranger in a Strange Land

Although Mallory MacLeod had no idea that, by nightfall, The Three Investigators would be talking about her on the porch of their cabin outside of Cool, a few hours before they thought about her, *she'd* been thinking about *them*. She'd been at the Scottish music camp in Grass Valley for fewer than three days, but already it seemed like forever. From morning to night there was fiddle music – incessant fiddle music, its notes jumping around like water skittering on a hot griddle. Mallory missed her life in Scotland a lot, but her mother had made a mistake in thinking she'd enjoy *this*.

She'd met one person she really liked at the camp – a shy Japanese girl named Hiroka who came from San Francisco and who spent much of her time rolling her eyes and covering her mouth with her hand so that no one could see her giggling. Hiroka had told Mallory her name meant "wise flower" – which Hiroka thought was hilarious. She spread her fingers around her face like petals and adopted an expression of serious ironic contemplation which

246

made Mallory laugh.

As it turned out, the campers came from all over California and most had a Scot somewhere in their past. She'd met Balfours and Campbells, Ramsays and MacGavins, MacClerys and MacHills. Somewhere there was probably a MacCheese. They were there because their parents had decided they needed "cultural enrichment." As a group, they were exceedingly earnest and super-nerdy, and although these were qualities Mallory often liked in people, it wasn't helping her to like the camp.

For one thing, the campers would scatter back to their homes all over California when the session was over, so there was little purpose in making friends with any of them, Mallory thought. For another, she'd never liked sticking out in a crowd, just as she'd explained to Bob Andrews. She hadn't said she was an introvert, but it was true. *He* was an introvert, as well, she thought – although his friend Pete Crenshaw was an extrovert if she'd ever met one.

If Jupiter Jones was the head of The Three Investigators, he must be an extrovert, too, Mallory thought. Bob had told her that Jupiter was a long-term planner, and very focused. Mallory knew that 'introvert' and 'extrovert' were terms created by a Swiss psychiatrist named Carl Jung, who had noticed that some of his patients were charged up by social interactions, while others – the introverts – often found them exhausting.

Boy, did they ever, Mallory thought. While most of her fellow campers seemed to like both talking and fiddle music, Mallory had always been unusually sensitive to what she considered irritating sounds, and if there was anything more irritating than a Scottish fiddle – or people *talking* about fiddling – she didn't know what it was.

In Scotland, when she'd started elementary school, she'd quickly been labeled a "bookworm," but she'd never really minded. Although a lot of people thought her reserved – or even snobbish – she really wasn't. She simply preferred to be alone with her books and her thoughts, if the alternative was living breathing people she often found ditchwater-dull.

That was part of why she missed her father so much – because he'd always been interesting to be with. Her father had been a natural leader and Mallory was a natural loner, but her father had also been her most important role model. Both he and she needed proof before believing things, and they both hated the kinds of rules and regulations made by anonymous bureaucrats in distant places.

In fact, while Mallory's mother disliked conflict and tended to make decisions driven by how she felt, both Mallory and her father tried to be logical and objective in the pursuit of truth. Though her father had been a lot thicker-skinned than Mallory was, he'd also been intensely curious – and a rebel in a lot of ways. He'd understood Mallory's rebellious streak because he shared it.

Unfortunately, Mallory's mother didn't understand her, even slightly. If she had, she'd never have brought her to Grass Valley. Mallory had told her she had no interest in attending a Scottish music camp, but Mrs. MacLeod simply hadn't listened.

As a result, right at this moment, Mallory and her mother were finishing dinner at this ghastly camp, and the camp director had just rung a bell to get the campers' attention. Every evening he reminded them that it was fire season and that they needed to be careful not to burn down the state of California – and sure enough, he reminded them again tonight. If only California *would* burn down, Mallory thought sardonically – then smiled at her own ridiculous thought.

Still, the place was certainly crowded, and although the area around Grass Valley was better than the area around Rocky Beach, California highways scared her. They were like ten normal highways jammed together in a roaring plain of noise.

"So what are you planning to do tonight? Are you going to the evening activity?" Mallory's mother asked as the servers started to clear away the dinner plates and bring out the desserts.

"I don't think so," Mallory said. "I'm trying to finish *Gulliver's Travels*. I took it out of the library thinking it was a fantasy, but as it turns out, it's more of a satire."

"Yes," her mother replied. "Have you gotten to the Yahoos yet?"

"Right now, I'm in Brobdingnag, where the people and plants and animals are totally gigantic," Mallory said. "Still, I looked ahead and saw a bit about the Yahoos. They reminded me of Skinny."

"Oh, Mallory, I know he's pretty terrible, but so far he's the only young person we know in Rocky Beach."

When Mallory's mother said things like this, it drove her absolutely crazy.

"He may be the only young person *you* know. I've met some others. The only problem is, they're boys," she said.

"But, Mallory, you *like* boys!" her mother said. "How could *that* be a problem? You've always made friends with boys more easily than with girls! Who are they, anyway?"

"Their names are Pete Crenshaw and Bob Andrews, and one of the reasons I like Bob, in particular, is that he doesn't hold it against me that I'm Skinny's cousin," Mallory said.

"Where did you meet these boys?" her mother asked. "Did Skinny introduce you?"

Mallory snorted. "Hardly," she said. "I was biking past a salvage yard with a painted fence around it when I decided to stop. Pete and Bob were there. Pete was the one I talked to. He seemed a bit pushy at first, but I think he may actually be pretty sensitive. I met Bob later. He told me that his friend Jupiter Jones, whose aunt and uncle own the salvage yard, had also lost his father."

"Jones?" her mother asked. "Is Jupiter Welsh?"

"I haven't met him, but it's weird you would ask me that," Mallory said. "When we lived in Scotland, I never thought about people's family backgrounds, but since we've arrived in California, I've almost *had* to – or at least to notice that *other* people seem to think about them a lot. That's why this camp is so successful. Still, any group *I* chose to join would be a group with *actual* shared interests, not phony-baloney ones."

A group like The Three Investigators, maybe, she thought to herself. Telling her mother that the boys she'd met were investigators would lead to all sorts of questions she either wouldn't want to answer or wouldn't be able to.

In the category of *wouldn't want to* would be the fact that, after Pete had given her the Three Investigators' business card, she'd gone home to her apartment in the Wessex House, settled herself at her desk, and plugged the words "The Three Investigators" into the search engine on her laptop. When she had, she'd found out quite a bit about Jupiter, Pete, and Bob.

She'd found, for example, that in one of their early cases, the theft of a parrot who had been taught to say "To-to-to be, or not to-to-to be," but who the boys had believed was stuttering, had led to the discovery of a beautiful lost painting. In another, The Three Investigators had met August August, an English boy who'd had to solve a mysterious message from his great-uncle Horatio in order to claim an inheritance – an inheritance which had turned out to be a famous and valuable Indian jewel called The Fiery Eye.

The thing about it was, when she was growing up in Scotland, Mallory herself had dreamed of solving puzzles. Her father had taught her about the history of Bletchley Park – an English estate that had housed the Government Code and Cypher School that had broken the German Enigma code during the Second World War – and though Mallory had no discernible talent for code-breaking, she genuinely wished she had.

Just then, the camp director rang the bell again – this time to announce that the evening activity would be a group game called Icons of Scotland, and that everyone who wanted to play should just stay in the dining room.

Her mother told Mallory she needed to do some work on her laptop in connection with a costume-designer movie job she'd be starting when they got back to Rocky Beach, but if Mallory wanted to stay and play the game, she'd be back to join her as soon as she could.

"I think I'd rather go back to the cabin

and read," Mallory told her.

However, before she could grab her backpack, Hiroka ran up to her and surprised her by suggesting they give the game a chance.

"It might be fun," she said.

"All right," said Mallory. "Let's try it."

The game, she found, was a memory game involving large cardboard flash cards the size of a poster. The players were divided into four teams; each team chose a team leader, and sat by themselves so they could talk out of the hearing of the other teams. A member of the camp's staff would then hold a flash card with a picture on top and a description on the bottom for two quick seconds – after which another staff member would step forward with another flash card.

The object was to remember what the icons were, and in what order they'd appeared, and when the team was ready to take a shot at an answer, the team leader shouted, "Ready!" then reported on the recollections of that team. Getting the right answer as quickly as possible was vital; according to what seemed quite a complex scoring system, three teams would eventually be disqualified, and the final team would win.

As the game began, the first sequence

involved only three cards, and Mallory listened as her team of ten campers argued with one another about what had happened when, and what the cards had shown.

She had always been able to remember things like this very easily, and by the time the staff had gotten to the seventh icon, her team's official leader had asked everyone else to shut up and just let Mallory do the work. One after another, everyone else in her group had been busy confusing the castles or forgetting the thistles or getting William Wallace and Robert Burns mixed up.

By the time they got to the twelfth card, there were only two teams left – Mallory's and another team with a member who had a talent similar to hers. Staff members flashed twelve cards at the last two teams – each for only two seconds. Since speed was important, the instant they were done, Mallory's team leader shouted "Ready!" and then nodded to Mallory to proceed.

Mallory sat and stared into the distance. She could see the so-called Icons as though they'd all been set up on easels before her. "Number one is the Falkirk Wheel," she said coolly. "Then Robert the Bruce. The Scottish thistle. Balmoral Castle." She took a deep breath. Many of the campers had gotten tripped up by the castles, confusing one with another, but she saw all their subtle differences as clear as day.

"Stirling Castle," she said. "A plate of haggis. Loch Ness. The Antonine Wall." The room had gotten very quiet. "Edinburgh Castle," Mallory said. "The Scottish Parliament. Robert Burns. And finally, our old friend Sean Connery."

"That's right!" the camp director announced.

The room erupted into whoops and applause, and Mallory's teammates crowded around her, jumping with excitement. Although she did not normally like to be the center of attention, Mallory felt touched by the enthusiasm of those surrounding her. She'd never thought of herself as someone who needed the approval of her fellows, but it felt good to have it, anyway.

She and her teammates all received rubber models of the greatest of Scottish icons, the Loch Ness monster − otherwise known as "Nessie" − and Mallory and Hiroka carried their prizes back to their seats with them. The monster had a long green neck and a small green head with reddish eyes and looked a lot like a brontosaurus. Still, in the aftermath of the applause, Mallory felt strangely fond of it.

After that, the fiddle music started. One note followed the other with giddy ferocity, and it was so relentless and so upbeat that, in spite of herself, Mallory found herself tapping her foot in time to the music. She nudged Hiroka and pointed.

"I can't stop it," Mallory whispered. "It's out of my control."

Hiroka looked amused, then spread her fingers around her face in "wise flower" posture and said, "Just say no."

Mallory and Hiroka's muted laughter brought the disapproving stares of the campers around them — which made the girls laugh harder. When the tune ended, Hiroka and Mallory said good night, still giggling a little. Back in the tiny cabin where they slept, Mallory found her mother working on her laptop.

"Oh, honey," she said. "I'm sorry I didn't make it back. What's that?" she asked when she saw Mallory's prize.

"Oh, Mom, how can you ask?" Mallory said. "My team won and we each got a Nessie. I like mine. In fact, I think she's brilliant."

She put the rubber model on a table, then threw herself onto her cot. There she pulled a book by Robert Heinlein down from her bedside table. It was a novel called *Stranger In A Strange Land*, and she'd already discovered that it told the story of a human who came to Earth in early adulthood, after being born on the planet Mars and raised by Martians.

As she lay holding the book above her chest, she found herself going back and forth between thinking about what she was reading and about her father, Callum MacLeod, who'd died so suddenly and unexpectedly. He really *had* understood her, but one of the things she missed the most was being able to understand *him*. He'd had a very commanding personality, but he'd also been creative – able to communicate the way he saw the world in such a way that it really energized his staff.

In fact, as an inventor, as well as an engineer, Callum MacLeod had always been on the lookout for new tools and new designs and new procedures. He'd also loved collaborating. He'd been a natural brainstormer, and when he and Mallory had talked together about the world, he'd helped her to see it more clearly. Since he'd died, she'd been in a sort of fog, and as she lay on the cot in the little cabin, considering her situation – and Gulliver's, and the hero of Heinlein's novel – tears started to well up in her eyes.

The truth was, she was exhausted – from the music and the game, from having giggled with Hiroka, from having been strangely touched by the applause when her team won, but most of all, from not having anyone in her life at the moment who she understood the way she'd understood her father. Even though her mother had promised that they would move back to Scotland in two years if Mallory couldn't get used to life in America, two years was a very long time, she thought.

She was about to turn over to hide her face when her mother sat down beside her and put her hand on Mallory's forehead.

"Mallory," she said. "What's wrong?"

"Oh, everything, Mom," Mallory said, wiping away her tears. "I miss Dad. And you know how much I like being alone. Up here I'm totally surrounded."

"I'm sorry," her mother said. "I thought this would be good for you, because you missed Scotland so much."

"Well, I do," Mallory said. "But that doesn't mean I miss 'The Bees of Maggieknockater.' I almost wish we were back in Rocky Beach. Or that school had started, or something. It's just the beginning of summer now, and I can't imagine what I'm going to do for the rest of it – especially once you go back to work. I wish we could at least get out of here for a while."

Her mother said, "We could go into Grass Valley tomorrow afternoon. Would you like that?"

"God, yes," Mallory said.

"If there's a bookstore in town, we could see if they have any books about the early history of California. The movie I'm going to be working on is about a woman whose husband was a leader of something called the Bear Flag Revolt."

"Do you want me to see if there *is* a bookstore?" Mallory said. When her mother nodded, she got up and went to her mother's laptop and in no time at all had discovered that there was a place called The Next Chapter Bookstore right in Grass Valley. It sold old books – no new ones – and from some photos taken inside the store, it also seemed to have some pretty cool pieces of antique furniture.

While her mother got ready for bed, Mallory studied several close-ups of a painted trunk for sale in The Next Chapter. It had an elegant wrought-iron handle on each end and an elaborate iron lock with a gigantic metal key. The front had three inset wooden panels. The lock and key were at the top of the central panel, and underneath them was painted the date 1845.

The left inset panel was painted with the name *Ebba Eriksdatter* and the right had a pedestal holding a vase with painted flowers. Mallory hoped the bookstore still had the trunk so she could see what was painted on the top and sides. But mostly she hoped that the name of the bookstore was a sign from the universe that she would soon find a way to close the current chapter of her life and move on to the next one.

Maybe on the way to the store she'd tell her mother a little more about The Three Investigators. By now they were supposed to be somewhere in the vicinity of Auburn – just a thirty minute drive from the Scottish music camp. But although Bob Andrews had suggested she call him while she was in Grass Valley, she felt funny about doing it for some reason she didn't entirely understand, but which probably involved not wanting to seem needy, or not feeling ready yet, or something along those lines.

Still, it was odd how easy it had been to talk with Bob when they'd met in the Rocky

Beach library, and when she thought back on her conversation with Pete Crenshaw, what she *really* remembered the most was his adorable lie about not being interested in cars.

The fact was, both Pete and Bob had seemed like great guys – and although Mallory hadn't met Jupiter Jones yet, when Bob had told her that he was good at explaining complicated stuff in a simple way and was also good at building things, she'd found herself wondering if he was anything like her father.

Of course, if he was the head of a firm called The Three Investigators, he probably wasn't a rebel, she reflected, but he probably wasn't merely an extrovert, either. He must be a real leader. Someone who had a natural urge to bring order and logic into the world around him.

Since Mallory had that urge herself, ever since Pete had given her the Three Investigators' business card she'd been thinking she might be able to help them out on a case sometime. After all, she'd always found novels in which detectives solved mysteries oddly consoling. Maybe she'd also find it consoling to help someone solve a mystery in real life – but from knowing how her father had run *his* company, Mallory also knew that if she were to have a chance of ever doing that, she would have to impress the head of *this* one right out of the gate.

For a moment, she wondered how she might do that, then decided that when she finally met Jupiter, she'd offer to shake his hand as if he were an adult. She'd recently read an article about greeting customs through the ages and had learned some interesting things about handshaking. In ancient Rome, two men would grab one another's forearms to make sure they had no knives up their sleeves, and in medieval Europe, knights shook hands to shake loose any hidden weapons.

Yes, that would do nicely, Mallory thought – though, of course, she could also ask Jupiter if he and the others had found gold up in the Gold Country, as Pete had hoped they would. As Mallory climbed into bed to get ready for sleep, she found herself wondering what The Three Investigators had actually been doing since they had left the town of Rocky Beach. Whatever it was, it had undoubtedly been more interesting and exciting than jumping around to fiddle music like a deranged grasshopper.

14

A Double Disappointment

As Worthington pulled the Range Rover into the parking lot of the Gold Country Historical Museum the following morning, Pete practically vibrated with excitement. They were on the verge of finding Li Chang's father's gold! Although it was terrible that he had been shot, it made more sense to Pete that it had happened because he'd found a lot of gold than because he was from China.

Of course, it was hard for Pete to understand why anybody would ever kill anybody except to protect their own life or the life of somebody they loved. The problem was, Li Chang's uncle, Hao Chang, might have claimed he was defending himself from Li Chang's father when he fired his pistol and shot him.

Still, as Pete bounded up the steps of the museum, his main feeling was that things were working out. That morning, he had his lucky rabbit's foot in his pocket again, and when they got into the museum, he touched it with his hand for luck as he saw that the woman they'd met the other day was again behind the wooden counter.

"Good morning, boys," she said. "I'm always glad to see repeat visitors. That means we've piqued your interest."

"That's for sure!" Pete said. "We're here because we'd like to see the book Li Chang got as a graduation prize."

At this, Jupiter took over the explanations. He said, "We met Gordon Small, who told us he'd donated a book that a student at the schoolhouse had won as a graduation prize. But we didn't see it in the glass case upstairs. It's a Greek primer called *Athena, Goddess of Wisdom*. Would you know where it is? We'd like to look at it."

The woman frowned. "That's a sore point, I'm afraid. I've been meaning to contact Mr. Small with the bad news."

"What bad news?" Bob asked.

"During a renovation a few months ago, we put the schoolhouse exhibit in storage, and some of the items were damaged. Carpenter ants tunneled into the pages of the primer, and it was so badly damaged we had to throw it away."

"Oh, no!" Pete said.

"That's most unfortunate," Jupiter said.

"We were really hoping to be able to look at it."

"Perhaps you can find a copy some-where else," the woman suggested.

"It was that particular copy we were hoping to look at," Jupiter said. "But thank you for your help."

What a roller coaster ride! Pete thought as they trooped back out to the Land Rover. No book, no pencil marks, no code, no noth-ing. They were right back at square one, and this time Jupiter seemed to have no ideas as to what to do about it.

In fact, he was standing and staring down the street in disappointment when Bob said, "Maybe we should go to Old Town and talk to Gordon Small. We haven't been back to see him since the day we met Connor, and even though we may have found out everything we can about Li Chang, we should still tell Mr. Small what happened to the book and thank him for his help."

"That's true," Jupiter said. "Let's go."

When they got to Old Town, Worthing-ton said he'd go for a walk and be back in half an hour. A waitress was working in Small's café today – a woman in her early twenties who had two blonde braids decorated with feathers.

When the boys saw that Gordon Small wasn't in his café, they settled at a table and ordered two Cokes and a root beer, then started to talk about the case. But in no time, the café door opened and Mr. Small came in. When he saw them, he came right over to their table.

"The Three Investigators!" he said. "Connor was filling me in this morning on your exploits. Why so down in the mouth? I thought you were close to success."

"We thought so, too," Jupiter said. "But we're not any more."

"Li Chang's book got eaten!" Pete said.

"What?" asked Mr. Small.

"Carpenter ants destroyed the pages," Bob said, "and the book was so badly damaged the museum had to throw it out."

"That really *is* a shame," Mr. Small said, "and not just because of the code you were hoping to find. Li Chang's book was a tangible piece of history – lost forever now. Well, you can't sit around feeling defeated. What do you say we take another peek in my attic in case I overlooked something?"

Pete thought this was nice of the man, but he didn't hold out much hope – and sure

267

enough, although Gordon Small's apartment was bright and sunny, filled with hanging ferns, and the attic was an interesting place, they found nothing new up there.

They did get to examine the ceiling joists and rafters and found it was constructed very solidly – its members fitted together not with nails, but with wooden pegs. Jupiter told them this construction method was called post and beam, or timber framing.

Back in the café they nursed their sodas and tried to re-group. Pete found himself staring at the talisman to ward off demons and saw that Jupiter was staring at it too.

"There's something not quite right about the print," Jupiter said. "But I can't figure out what it is."

"It just looks different because of the angle," Pete offered. "Remember it was hung much higher in the Salvage Yard."

"And the light was much better," Bob said. "It's dim in here."

"Hmm," Jupiter said. "I wonder if Mr. Small would let us take it down so I can see it more clearly."

Gordon Small had no objection and even got a stepladder to help the boys. Pete climbed up, unhooked it from the hangers that held it, and brought it down.

"Now hold it over there," Jupiter said, "so the light from the front windows shines directly on it."

Pete held the talisman, front side out, toward Jupe, who stood in the doorway of the café, his arms crossed, studying the print. Pete found himself staring at the back of the talisman. Something had been written in a spidery script on the canvas — a list of sorts, stretching from close to the top all the way to the bottom. Pete squinted and looked closer and to his utter astonishment saw a long line of paired numbers, separated by dashes.

"Guys," he said, his voice rising. "You're not going to believe this! Remember the last thing Li Chang said to his wife before he died?"

"The demons, the demons," Jupiter said.

Pete flipped the talisman around.

"Look at that!" he cried exultantly.

"Wow!" Bob said. "The code."

Pete started waving the talisman around in the air in jubilation.

"Careful with that," Jupiter said. "We need it more than ever now."

"What's going on?" Mr. Small said, and Jupiter explained what they'd found.

"Oh no!" Pete suddenly said. "Before,

we thought we had the book and no code, but now we have the code and no book.”

“That should be all right,” Jupiter said. “All we need now is another copy of the same edition of the book. It doesn’t matter that we don’t have Li Chang’s copy – which he might or might not have left visible marks in. We’ll never know now. But presuming this is the code, any copy of the book will work to let us decode the cipher.”

Bob had begun copying down the numbers very carefully and Jupe was checking them. No mistakes – they couldn’t afford a single one. When Bob was finished, the boys helped Gordon Small hang the print up again; while they worked, they wondered how long it would take to find another copy of Li Chang’s book. They would need to be starting back for Rocky Beach soon, and Pete didn’t see how they could possibly solve the book cipher before they left.

“Maybe I can help you by looking online,” Gordon Small said. “After all, you’re going to need the exact same edition of the book, and I know what the cover of it looked like. Of course, it would also have to have been published prior to 1873, when Li Chang graduated.”

He invited them over to his computer, and in a few keystrokes he was on a large site that tied together book dealers from around the world.

He typed in the title of Li Chang's prize and scrolled through pictures of various editions. It turned out to have been a pretty popular book, back when Greek was routinely studied.

But only one edition − from the 1870s − had the cover Mr. Small remembered. The cloth was a deep royal blue, the title was stamped across the top in gold italic letters, and in the exact center of the cover was a small owl, looking wise and a bit forlorn.

"That's it," Mr. Small said. "And look! There's a copy in a used bookstore up in Grass Valley, about a half hour from here. Do you want me to call them and have them hold it for you?"

"That's a good idea," said Jupiter. "Though I doubt there's a run on that particular book."

After Gordon Small had called the store, Bob wrote down the address and phone number in his notebook.

Just then Worthington came back. When Jupiter filled him in, he was keen to head up

Highway 49. Before they left, Pete gave his walkie-talkie to Gordon Small.

"We'll only be thirty miles away, Mr. Small," he said, "and these are supposed to have a range of fifty miles. But thirty miles will be a good test. Do you mind if we call you on it when we're up in Grass Valley to make sure it works? We can let you know we got the book."

"That's fine, Pete," Gordon Small said. "Happy to help in any way I can. Roger that."

He gave Pete a mock salute.

As they headed out of town, past the strip malls and shopping centers, Pete had to wonder at how quickly life could turn around. One minute you were full of hope and the next your hopes were dashed. But right around the corner a surprise was waiting which could fill you full of hope again. And though there were plenty of people in the world like John Chang, there were also people like Gordon Small and Connor O'Malley – strangers who'd quickly become their friends and who'd helped them out when they'd needed it.

As they left Auburn behind, the double-laned highway became a two-way road, and the land turned more rural – golden grass-covered fields with stands of live oaks where a couple of horses grazed – and, as the elevation climbed, it became more rocky and mountainous. As they entered Grass Valley the highway widened again into several lanes.

"That's the exit," Pete pointed out. "Downtown Grass Valley."

Worthington got off, and the road meandered past a small outcrop of fast-food shops and a long stretch of irrigated field. But soon they entered the business district and Bob used the GPS to direct Worthington to Elm Street. Worthington parked the Land Rover and the four of them got out. Down the street they could see the storefront. The large glass windows held the store's name in gilt letters in a graceful arc, and under The Next Chapter Bookstore were the words "Used and Old Books. No New Books."

Inside, the place was warm and smelled of dust and pulp and sunlight. Colorful maps and prints covered the exposed brick walls and old schoolhouse lights hung from the very high ceiling on elongated posts. The store was crowded with books – books in stacks on the floor, books heaped in interesting old steamer trunks, leaning in teetering piles against the walls, and long metal rows of shelves that looked like the ones in the Rocky Beach Library.

Though it wasn't an antique store, there were a number of old pieces of furniture – a painted trunk with wrought-iron handles, a wing-backed chair upholstered in a bright print, several glass-fronted cupboards and bookcases which actually held books.

Pete noticed that Bob had crouched down in front of the painted trunk, and when he looked at it over Bob's shoulder, he saw that on the top were two painted boxes holding a pedestal with painted flowers, while the front displayed the name *Ebba Eriksdatter* and the date 1845.

"Why's that date on it?" he asked Bob.

"I guess that must have been the year it was made," Bob said.

It was quiet and the boys were standing, letting their eyes adjust to the light, when a woman emerged from between the rows of shelves. A pair of glasses hung on her chest from a chain around her neck.

"I didn't hear you come in," she said cheerily. "I keep meaning to have some bells put on the door so I get some warning."

"We're here to pick up a book," Bob said. "Our friend Gordon Small called you about a half hour ago. *Athena, Goddess of*

Wisdom?"

"Why yes," the woman said. "And I'm glad he called ahead. It's taken me almost all that time to find it. My filing system's a bit – well, you can see." She swept her hand around at the clutter, then held out a copy of the book they'd been after. "A good clean copy," she said. "From a private collection. Not ex-library."

Pete felt the back of his neck prickle with anticipation. "Lucky for us you like books!" he said.

The woman looked at him with interest. "Yes," she said.

They moved toward the desk where the woman kept a small cash box, and Jupiter was paying for the book when Pete heard a vaguely familiar voice, tinged with surprise, say, "Hello. What are *you* doing here?"

All four of them turned in the direction of the voice. Pete was surprised to see Mallory MacLeod emerging from between the shelves of books, followed by a woman Pete guessed must be her mother. Mallory looked really happy to see Bob, Pete thought. And gosh, was she pretty.

Bob seemed to think so, too, if his smile was anything to go by.

"Mallory!" he said. "I was just saying you were in Grass Valley!"

"I was going to call you later today," she said. "I'm sorry I didn't do it before, but the fiddle music has made it hard to think. Mom, these are the boys I told you about. Pete Crenshaw." She nodded in Pete's direction. "And Bob Andrews. This is my mother, Alexandra MacLeod."

Pete and Bob both shook her hand. Then Bob said to Mallory's mother, "And this is Jupiter Jones."

"How do you do, Jupiter," said Mrs. MacLeod.

They, too, shook hands. Then Mallory stepped forward holding out her hand, too. "I understand you're the mastermind behind The Three Investigators," she said respectfully.

Jupiter was not often caught off-guard, but Pete could see this was one of the rare times.

Jupiter swallowed as Mallory took his hand and shook it. "I'm happy to finally meet you," she said. "I recently read an article about greeting customs through the ages. I learned that shaking hands signals trust, since neither of the parties can be holding a weapon." She smiled slightly, looking at Jupiter squarely.

Jupiter looked back at her with sudden interest. "A little-known fact these days. But in medieval Europe, knights routinely engaged in the practice in order to shake loose any weapons that might be hidden," he said.

"Yes," said Mallory. "I believe the Greeks did it first. During the Roman era, it involved two men grabbing one another's forearms to make sure they had no knives up their sleeves."

"Of course, in many Asian countries, people just bow to each other when meeting," said Jupiter.

"And the Eskimos rub noses!" Pete interjected. He thought with some satisfaction that he'd been right when he'd told Jupiter that he thought Jupe would actually *like* Mallory – and that Bob had been right when he'd told him that Jupiter and Mallory had more in common than Jupiter might think.

"It's nice to see you again, Pete," Mallory said, then turned to Bob. As Mallory swung her head around, her hair swung with her; Pete thought he had never seen red hair of such an attractive shade.

"Have you found out anything further about your client's ancestor?" Mallory asked Bob. "You said he ran a laundry in Auburn, but there were rumors that his father was killed for a bag of gold, and that Pete hoped the gold was still there somewhere.”

“You told her *that*?” Pete said. Bob was normally pretty close-mouthed when it came to their cases, but this time he’d thrown caution to the winds. Though the reason couldn’t have been more obvious, Bob confirmed it, anyway, with what he said next.

“We’ve been to the laundry. It’s a café now – Small’s Café – but it’s in the same building where Li Chang ran his business,” he explained to Mallory. “He was really quite interesting. His father and mother both came to California during the Gold Rush. His mother was Irish, and his father was Chinese. I’ve started to identify with him a little, for obvious reasons. Maybe you could come down to Auburn before we go back to Rocky Beach. You know that talisman in the Salvage Yard you were staring at? The exact same one is hanging in the café in Auburn!"

"And there's a secret code written on the back of it!" Pete said, not to be outdone. "The book we came up to Grass Valley to get – " He pointed in the direction of the woman's desk. " – holds the key."

"A book cipher?" Mallory said. "Wow!"

"You know about those?" Pete said. "Maybe you can help us solve it!"

"I think the three of us should do that at the cabin," Jupiter said meaningfully. "Tonight, after we get back there," he added in the same tone. As both Pete and Bob were well aware, Jupiter had never had much use for girls.

"That's all right," Mallory said. "But I'd love to come down to Auburn and see the other copy of the Talisman Against Demons."

"I could drive you down tomorrow," said Mrs. MacLeod helpfully.

"I'd love that," Mallory said.

"What time should we meet you?" Bob asked. "Would 11:00 work for you? At Small's Café?"

Mallory looked at her mother, who nodded. They all said goodbye, but as the boys were waiting for the bookstore owner to put their book in a bag, Mallory walked over to the painted trunk that Pete and Bob had examined when they came in.

"Oh, look," she said to her mother. "The Scandinavian immigrant's trunk I saw online! Here's the owner's name and the date she came to America. It's fantastic. I love the painted boxes at both ends and on the top. It all looks original – even the wrought-iron strapping on the back."

Bob and Pete watched as Mallory and her mother left the store, and after they were gone, Bob went back to the trunk to take some pictures of it with his phone. Although Pete didn't know exactly why he was doing this, he didn't want to ask, but after they left the bookstore and clambered into the Land Rover, he suddenly remembered that they had planned to use this trip to test the walkie-talkies.

"Bob," he said. "Hand me your walkie-talkie. I want to contact Mr. Small."

He pressed the button and the connection crackled. "Mr. Small, are you there?" he said. "Over." He turned to his friends. "I hope the channel didn't get changed or something."

And then they could all hear Gordon Small's voice. "I'm here, Pete," he said. "You're coming through loud and clear. Did you get the book? Over."

"We sure did, Mr. Small. We're just about to start back to Auburn to decipher the message. Thanks a lot. Over and out." He handed the walkie-talkie back to Bob. "That sure worked fine."

"A good piece of equipment," Jupiter said approvingly. "We didn't need the fifty-mile range on this case, but at some point in the future, we might."

He had a look in his eye, Pete thought, that suggested he was thinking about something other than walkie-talkies, and sure enough, once they were about to get back on the highway, Jupiter proved as impatient as Pete was to get on with solving the coded message.

"On second thought," Jupiter said, "I see no advantage in putting off what we've gone to such trouble to discover. I saw a sign for some fairgrounds. Worthington, could you please turn right up ahead?"

It was just a short distance to the fairgrounds, and in no time, Worthington had parked the Land Rover in the shadow of towering pines and the four of them were sitting at a picnic table with the book they'd just purchased in front of Jupiter.

Bob had opened his notebook to the code, then handed it to Pete, who read out the numbers while Jupiter turned the pages of the book and counted the words, and Bob wrote down the slowly emerging message.

The first three words were "*My dearest wife.*"

"Wow!" Pete said. "It's like a message from the great beyond!"

"Or something like that," Jupiter agreed. "Next numbers, please."

Flipping the pages and carefully counting the words took time and diligence, and more than once Jupiter had to stop and start again.

"We don't want to get anything wrong," he said, moving his finger along the lines of text. "Thank goodness he only used the English pages."

Bob's back was tense as he sat, waiting for the next word. As he wrote down each one, he pressed so hard it seemed he was carving the letters into the paper. Pete couldn't believe how calm Jupiter seemed.

There were a lot of numbers, and the message was getting longer.

"If you are reading these words, then I have died before I could retrieve my father's gold from the place where the truest treasure resides."

"Where the truest treasure resides?" Pete said. "He hid it in a bank?"

"I don't think so," Jupiter said. "Let's keep working."

"My plan at the moment is to retrieve the gold and use it to ease our old age after my mother's curse has been cleansed by time."

"But he died in the flu epidemic and never lived to be really old!" Pete said.

"If I am dead by that time, then you must re-claim the gold, and, if not you, then our son or his sons or daughters. The gold must go to a direct descendant of my honored father."

"That means Isabella Chang!" Bob said. "Wait 'til she hears about this!"

"Perhaps we should discover the gold," Jupiter said mildly, "before we tell Ms. Chang she's rich."

The boys were working feverishly now.

"You will find it in a leather pouch, in the wonderful library where I have spent so many hours."

"The library," Worthington said. "Where the truest treasure resides."

"Yes," Jupiter said. "All the clues led in the same direction right from the start."

"It is hidden in a secret pocket in the floor, in a timber my friend who helped build the library salvaged from an old barn he and I played in as children."

"That barn must have been built with timber framing," Jupiter said. "That means the carpenter used mortis and tenon construction − like the attic of Gordon Small's café. He'd have cut a hole in a beam where a large square peg from a post or an adjoining beam slid in. It sounds like Li Chang found a mortis hole and put the gold into it. Ingenious!"

"My friend knew the timber would be at least as

strong as the other joists, and he wanted to connect the time when we were students at Angus O'Malley's school, and the time when the library was being built."

"Wow," Bob said. "He would have liked your aunt and uncle's salvage yard, Jupiter. Though his use of the timber was symbolic."

"An astute observation," said Worthington.

"My friend is dead now, but he would not object to my use of his timber as a hiding place. You will find the joist quite easily, once you look."

They were getting near the end now. Pete scanned down the column of numbers.

"Once there, take up the floor board, pry out the plug in the timber, and lift out the leather envelope."

"We're so close!" Pete said. "I can hardly stand it!"

"Goodbye, dearest wife. Just go to the spot I have marked on the map."

"What map?" Pete whispered.

They all stopped talking and stared at each other in dismay.

A half hour later, they were back in their cabin, all of them pretty glum. They cooked dinner and ate it in silence, and afterwards Jupiter suggested that maybe it was time to call Isabella Chang after all. Pete thought Jupe had been right the first time – that it would have been a lot more satisfying if they could tell her that by the following evening she would be rich. Still, Pete understood why Jupiter wanted to let her know what was going on.

In the end, it was Bob who called her. He turned the volume on his cellphone all the way up, then punched Isabella Chang's number and put the phone on the table as they sat hunched around it. She picked up quickly, and Jupiter took over.

"Good evening, Ms. Chang," Jupiter said. "This is Jupiter Jones calling."

"Jupiter!" Isabella Chang said. "I've been waiting to hear from you!"

"Pete and Bob and I are still up in Auburn," Jupiter said. "We've been hot on the case for several days now, and we've almost achieved success."

"I had every confidence in you," Ms. Chang said. "I knew that Hector wouldn't lead me astray."

"We've found out a lot about Li Chang," Jupiter said, "but the most important news is that Li's father wasn't murdered because he was Chinese. Li's father died because of the gold he had found, and Li hid his father's treasure in the Carnegie Library in Auburn."

Pete sat forward eagerly, waiting to hear

Isabella Chang's response.

But there was no response. For a moment he thought the call had been disconnected. Then Isabella spoke, her voice hesitant and more quiet. "I – I hardly know what to say."

It took some time for Jupiter to fill her in on everything that had happened, but in the end he got the job done. He told her about the trail of clues they'd followed, and what they had learned from them – that Hao Chang had shot Li Chang's father, perhaps by accident; that John Chang was Hao's direct descendent; that the book cipher stated that the gold should go to Li Chang's lineal descendants; that her cousin John Chang was in monetary trouble and, from the start, had been trying to deflect and dissuade as he worked to get his hands on the gold; and, finally, that they were in search of a map that would lead them to the spot in the library where the gold had been hidden. Finally, Jupiter admitted that he feared they'd never discover the map.

Isabella's voice grew harsh. "John Chang!" she said. "I never liked the man. I should have known he couldn't be trusted. I'm usually a good judge of character, but – "

"After all," Jupiter said. "He's family,

and one does tend to make allowances – "

"Yes," Isabella Chang said. "Even when they are not deserved."

"I hope we can call you again soon with better news," Jupiter said. "We have to find the map."

"You'll find it," Isabella Chang said confidently. "I know you will. And if it leads you to the gold I never believed existed, ten percent of it will be yours, as a reward for all the work you've done."

Pete sat back in his chair and stared at his friends. Bob looked very surprised. Jupiter, of course, gave little away.

"That's very kind of you, Ms. Chang," Jupiter said, "but perhaps you should wait until the gold is indeed yours and you see how much it is worth."

"Prudent advice," Ms. Chang said. "But one way or another, you boys are due a finder's fee if you manage to discover the treasure."

Jupiter said they'd call her soon and pressed the END button.

"Boy," Pete said, "I wish I felt as confident as she did."

"I wish I did, too," Jupiter said.

Still, Pete was glad they'd called. And as

he climbed into the top bunk in the bedroom of the cabin, ready to go to sleep, he felt quite bucked up. After all, even though Jupiter hated to hear anyone say it, he was a genius. This had caused some of his classmates to call Jupiter "Genius Jones" when he was younger – and not entirely as a compliment. In fact, not as a compliment at all. Maybe that was the reason why he hated to hear the word applied to him.

But though Jupiter got almost all his satisfaction in life from thinking his way through problems, he also knew how to work with other people. In fact, when Jupiter, Pete, and Bob put their heads together, Pete thought they could do just about anything.

15

Hiding in Plain Sight

The next morning, Jupiter lay on a large flat rock in the middle of the North Fork of the American River, a few miles outside of Auburn. His eyes were closed, but he could sense the bright orange disc of the sun hovering above him.

The boys had had extra time that morning before they were supposed to meet Mallory MacLeod at Gordon Small's café, and Pete – who had looked longingly at the ribbon of the river winding in the canyon every time he'd seen it – had convinced them to take a quick swim on the way into town. Because Worthington had had to park the Land Rover very close to the highway, he'd decided to stay with the car, and the boys had run down the steep trail leading to the river.

Even in summer, the water was very cold. When Jupiter had first jumped in, he'd had to keep himself from yelling at the shock, but after he'd pulled himself up and out of the water, the tingling in his skin was very pleasant as the sun took the chill out of him. It almost felt as though he were melting into the stone.

Pete and Bob were nearby, laughing and shouting, splashing each other and diving from a rock they repeatedly climbed up on into the turquoise pool at its base. Jupiter marveled at how carefree they were. Though they were as disappointed as he was that the book cipher had not led them to the gold, they'd been able to put it out of their minds for a time. He, however, had not.

He thought – and not for the first time – that the restless obsessive nature of his intellect was a mixed blessing. On the one hand, it allowed him to concentrate on a problem – to keep at it and at it until he found a way through it. On the other hand, it rarely allowed him to let go and enjoy the simpler things in life as completely as Pete and Bob did – and right now, he found himself a little annoyed that he hadn't found a way to object to the suggestion that Mallory MacLeod come down to Auburn and see the talisman in Small's Café.

Of course, he'd liked her a lot more than he'd expected to, and he smiled a little grimly at the memory of the two of them shaking hands while they verbally dueled about the history of that particular social custom. She'd held her own. She was smart, and she seemed to know a good deal.

Nevertheless, the upcoming meeting had been arranged at a moment when it had seemed that The Three Investigators were inches away from the problem's solution and that they'd have the satisfaction of laying out the clues to Mallory and explaining how they'd discovered the gold when they met again.

But although Jupiter now knew where Li Chang had hidden it, and who it belonged to, he still had no idea where in the library it was – and even though Isabella Chang had seemed very confident that if they'd gotten this far, they would get all the way, Jupiter wasn't so sure about that at all.

Besides, seeing Mallory would be merely a social event, and time was very much on Jupiter's mind. They had already been on the road for four days – today was day five – and they had planned to take two days to drive back to Rocky Beach, starting the following morning.

Worthington needed to get the Land Rover back to the Rent-'n'-Ride the day after tomorrow, at the latest, and – as an added worry for Jupiter – when Worthington drove away from the Salvage Yard to deliver the car to his boss, The Three Investigators would be losing both their car and their driver in one fell swoop.

Of course, if they found the gold, Isabella Chang had promised them a reward. Until she had mentioned that on the phone, Jupiter had been completely uninterested in the treasure for its own sake. It had been pleasurable to get a reward for finding the Fiery Eye, some time back, but he hadn't set up an investigative firm in order to become rich. It was the application of the logical processes of his mind to a difficult problem – the ability to see possibilities where others did not, to think his way around dark corners – that Jupiter most enjoyed.

Now, though, he was thinking that if they somehow *could* find the gold, the reward might be enough for them to be able to afford a secondhand car. It might even be enough for them to be able to pay Worthington to drive them around for a while. Where could the map be? Had it been in the one-room schoolhouse, he wondered, and now was irretrievably lost? Could it be hiding somewhere in the attic above where the laundry had been? He didn't think so – they'd looked quite hard the day before and had found nothing. Could it be in the library itself?

He needed space and quiet to contemplate these questions, but gloomily he understood that it would be several hours before he was able to get any such thing – because Pete and Bob were determined to show Mallory the sights. They wanted her not only to see Gordon Small's café, but also Connor's studio at the library – which, under the circumstances, made Jupiter even more irritated. To be so close to the gold and yet to have no clear idea where it was – His friends even wanted to take Mallory to the museum to show her Li Chang's plaque, but he thought at least he'd be able to put a stop to that.

"Hey, Jupe," Pete yelled. "Come on in. The water's fine!"

Jupiter raised his head from the rock. It was feeling very heavy; he found that thinking in the warmth of the sun suited him. He waved his hand, a gesture of dismissal so slight that both Pete and Bob laughed and went back to their swimming.

For days now Jupiter had had the feeling that he was missing something – that his normally very finely tuned powers of observation were letting him down. There was something he didn't know that he ought to know, but he didn't know what it was. As well, he felt an acute sense of responsibility – both to Isabella Chang and to Bob.

The night before – after the conversation with Isabella Chang – Bob had told him about his great idea of writing up their cases using alliterative alphabetical titles, and if Jupiter couldn't figure out where the gold was and bring this case to a successful conclusion, Bob wouldn't even be able to write it up.

While half a loaf might be better than none, Jupiter thought, half a case was of no use to anyone. It just wouldn't interest enough people. People were looking for a satisfying conclusion.

Although Jupiter assumed that the old Carnegie Library was owned by the town of Auburn, and that The Three Investigators could (theoretically) approach someone who worked for City Hall and ask their help in searching, he knew enough about governments to know that it would probably take a year before his request was even considered.

On top of all that, Jupiter was quite frustrated with himself for not having figured out, all on his own (without the coded message) that if the gold had existed, it would have *had* to be hidden in the library. Not only was FREE TO ALL carved on Li Chang's gravestone, but Jupiter had been thinking for days that the study of character was the linchpin of all good detective work, and he knew as well as he knew anything that if you could see to the hearts and minds of the people involved in a case, all would become clear.

But had he remembered that at the proper instant? No, he hadn't. If he had, he would have put together the details in Li Chang's graduation poem with the volunteer work he'd done for the library and the reverence he had for books – a reverence so great that he himself had kept a small library in the laundry to lend to his customers – and would have seen that Li would naturally have hidden the gold in a place he already valued deeply – a place where books were found.

Jupiter sat up and rubbed his eyes. The sun was very hot – so hot he was feeling a bit sleepy. He pressed his thumb against his chest and saw that it turned white when he released it – a sure sign he was close to getting burned. He looked at his watch. It was almost 10:30. Pete and Bob were now doing as he had done – lying on rocks, spread-eagled, soaking up the rays, as Pete would say.

"Guys," Jupiter said. "Look at the time. We'd better get going." Bob and Pete groaned and sat up. Jupiter slipped into the river, and this time he yelled. He swam as fast as he could for shore and was drying himself off when he was joined by Pete and Bob. All three dressed, and after rolling their swimsuits in their towels, they began the trudge up the steep trail to Worthington and the Land Rover. They were halfway there when Jupiter heard a series of thuds and looked up to see a boulder bouncing down the trail, coming straight at them.

"Look out!" he yelled. "Into the brush."

All three of them hurried off the trail and stood watching the rock as it went hurtling past. It landed in the river with a huge splash.

"Quiet!" Jupiter said, and all three of them stood as still as possible. Jupiter heard a scuffling – the sound of someone making his way through the brush.

"I think someone rolled a rock down on us," he said.

"Maybe it was an accident," Pete said.

"Maybe," Jupiter said. "But maybe not." They soon met up with Worthington who said only that he'd seen a man walking on the highway, nothing suspicious. Still, all the way into Auburn, Jupiter kept turning around and staring out the back window. He had the oddest feeling that they were being followed, and even after Worthington had parked, and Jupiter and Pete and Bob had gone into Small's Cafe, he couldn't shake the feeling.

"Boys!" Gordon Small said, coming over to their table. "How's everything?" He put Pete's walkie-talkie down in front of him with a thump. Jupiter smiled dimly and stared up at the Talisman Against Demons. He remained quiet as Pete and Bob told Gordon what had happened.

"A map?" Gordon said. "Well, I never found a map when I took over the building. Not downstairs or in the living area upstairs, not even in the attic."

Mallory MacLeod was right on time, 11 o'clock sharp. A good sign, Jupiter thought. She opened the door to the café and stood there silhouetted by the morning light before she spotted them and walked over.

"Hi," she said. "My mom's walking around Old Town, checking it out. I think even *she* was glad to get away from the endless fiddle music."

When a waitress came over, Mallory ordered coffee, and when the waitress left, Pete erupted into speech.

"Look. Up there!" he said, pointing toward the wall. "An exact copy of one of the talismans in the Salvage Yard. What do you think of that for coincidence?"

Mallory looked up at it for a minute, then slowly but firmly shook her head. "I don't think it's a coincidence at all," she said.

"What do you mean?" asked Bob. "If it's not a coincidence, what is it?"

"What I mean is that *isn't* a copy of the one in Rocky Beach," Mallory said. "It's totally different. Well, not totally. The Chinese man with the little green crown is the same. But the bottom half? The one down in Rocky Beach looked sort of like a pagoda with squiggles and lines inside, and something that resembled a Chinese character. In this one, the bottom half looks sort of like a – well, like a map."

"A map!" Pete exclaimed in high excitement.

"It *does* look like a map!" Bob almost shouted. "And look! At the back there's a small cross!"

Jupiter, too, felt almost like shouting. Of course. That was what had been nagging at him. The bottom half of the talisman above him was subtly different from the one his uncle had brought home. There were long rectangular boxes lined up inside a bigger box, with fancy curved lines at the edges that now looked merely like decorations. The boxes looked a bit like the well-arranged and serried shelves of books in a library. And there, at the end of one of the shelves, right in the back corner, was a small cross. Could that be where Connor's studio was?

Jupiter listened while Pete and Bob excitedly explained to Mallory what the book cipher had revealed – and what it hadn't – and also told her that the coded numbers had been discovered on the back of the talisman.

"But I really don't see how you knew right away that the talismans were different," Bob said to Mallory, admiringly.

"I've got a good memory in general," she responded. "But when it comes to material culture, it's *really* good."

"What's material culture?" Pete said curiously.

"Things created by people," Mallory said. "Cars, buildings, clothing, art and artifacts, and tools."

"Well, it's lucky for us you have that kind of memory. We should go to the library right now!" Pete said. "I bet Connor O'Malley will be there! If he is, he can help us find the gold."

"He never gave us his number, but maybe Gordon Small can call and tell him we're on our way," Bob said.

"Would you like to come with us?" Jupiter asked Mallory politely. Although he wasn't ready to decide whether or not he really liked her or was just grateful to her for contributing such a crucial observation at such a crucial moment, he knew it would be extremely rude not to include her in the next – and final – stage of the investigation.

"I'd love to," Mallory said. "I just have to call my mother and tell her where I'll be." She pulled out a flip-top cellphone a lot like Bob's and made the call – then told the waitress she wouldn't want the coffee, after all.

In the meantime, Gordon Small called Connor O'Malley. Bob took a picture with his phone and also drew a careful replica of the figure on the bottom of the talisman – as big as he could make it – on a single sheet of paper. You couldn't be too careful. The four of them then piled into the Land Rover, along with Worthington – and when Pete gallantly offered Mallory the front passenger seat he'd been occupying since they left Rocky Beach, Mallory accepted. On the way to the library, over and amid his excitement, Jupiter couldn't shake the feeling, again, that they were being followed.

But although he kept looking over his

shoulder, he could see nothing except for normal traffic. On Almond Street they all got out and hurried up the concrete steps, under the architrave, and through the front door of the old library. Jupiter held the copy of the map Bob had made and pointed out what he thought were the lines indicating the concrete steps and the one that stood for the front door.

"Look," he pointed out.

A curved line swept from near the door away and to the side.

"Maybe the circulation desk?" he said. "And this box here. Maybe the old card catalogue?"

The place was quiet and seemed deserted until they heard Connor's voice.

"Is that you, boys?" he said.

"And a girl. And Worthington," Pete said.

The five of them hurried to join Connor.

"Hello, Worthington. Who's this?" he said with pleasure – at which Bob introduced Mallory.

Jupiter quickly filled Connor in, showing Connor the replica of the map that Bob had drawn. He pointed to the cross and said he believed they should be searching in the room's back corner where a box of supplies and a stack of paintings stood against the wall.

"Well, look at that!" Connor said, when the stuff had been moved. The five of them huddled together on their hands and knees on the wide pine boards.

"The whole floor's been nailed," Connor said. "Except for this one board. I never noticed that before."

He'd taken a directional light from a worktable and put it on the floor. Jupiter could see the small section of flooring where the two walls came together. One of the wide pine boards had been top-screwed, with the screw heads visible as black dots with straight lines through them.

"If this is where Li hid the gold," Jupiter said. "I bet he took up the board some time when he was alone in the library – "

"He probably had a key," Bob said. "He did volunteer work and he could have gotten in at night."

Jupiter continued. "And instead of nailing it back down, he screwed it. He may have been afraid that if he nailed it again, the board would split."

From his pocket he took his Swiss Army knife and flipped open the screwdriver. Around him he could feel the tension rising as he began to unscrew the board. When the final screw had been removed, Jupiter lifted the board out, and Connor shone the bright light into the hole. Jupiter and the others found themselves looking at a substantial timber about twelve inches wide. There was nothing else to be seen.

"Oh, no!" Pete said. "Here we go again."

"Remember the coded message," Jupiter said. He pointed to a rectangular block of wood, slightly lighter in color than the beam in which it was set.

"Li put a plug in the hole to keep his hiding place safe," he said.

He reached into the hole and poked the blade of his Swiss Army knife into the line between the lighter and darker wood, working it back and forth until he'd created some space. Then, using the blade as a lever, he pried the plug loose. It popped up and they could all see the original mortise hole − and inside it a flat leather pouch covered with dust.

Above him, Jupiter could hear five quick intakes of breath as he reached down and pulled the dusty leather out. It was surprisingly heavy, and he could see why Li Chang had called it an envelope; it was four inches wide by seven inches long, with a thickness of no more than an inch and a half. A tongue covered the front part. It was adorned with Chinese characters, and tied securely down, so that it was impossible to look inside the pouch without untying it.

The expressions on the others' faces as Jupiter stood up holding the pouch were very gratifying – exaltation, intense interest, surprise, and pleasure. Jupiter shifted the envelope so that he was holding it on both his palms.

"I wouldn't be surprised," Jupiter said, "if there were twenty pounds of gold here – or more."

Pete looked at the pouch balanced across Jupiter's hands. "But it's so small!" he said.

"The same amount of two different things can have very different weights," Mallory said. "Think of a bar of butter versus a bar of lead."

"I've never held a bar of lead!" Pete said.

The others gathered around one of Connor's tables as Jupiter set the pouch down and unfastened the leather thongs. It was hard to be certain, but Jupiter thought there might be as many as fifty or sixty dull gold nuggets, crammed tightly together inside. On top of the nuggets was a folded piece of paper. Jupiter opened it and read it aloud.

"*Last Will and Testament of Li Chang,*" he read. "*I bequeath this gold, inherited from my mother, Rose Chang, to my direct descendent or descendants. Li Chang. In Auburn, California. August 15, 1917.*"

"Wow!" Pete said.

Carefully, Jupiter slipped Li Chang's *Last Will and Testament* back into the pouch. Wow, indeed. He had just finished tying the envelope up again when he heard some stealthy footsteps.

He and the others turned to find they were face to face with John Chang and the Chinese man the boys had seen at the Historical Society meeting. The man grinned malevolently. He was holding a short length of pipe – a menacing-looking object, held in a menacing way. In a steady rhythm he beat it against his palm.

Worthington pointed at him. "You're the man I saw on the highway earlier this morning," he said angrily.

"That was an accident," John Chang said dismissively. "We were simply trying to see what they – and you – were doing in my town."

Chang held his hand out to Jupiter.

"I'll take that," he said, "with thanks

from the Gold Country Historical Society. We've been looking for that for some time now."

Jupiter looked at him. Clearly he had fooled Chang with his earlier efforts to act less intelligent than he was, but this time, he made no such effort.

"I believe you about the boulder being an accident – because having us alive and un-injured was your only hope for discovering where Li Chang had hidden his gold," he said. "If you'd been as smart as you think you are, you'd have figured out earlier that The Three Investigators are not as easily fooled as you wanted to believe. And if you think you can steal Li Chang's gold, think again."

Chang drew himself up and sneered. "As you may not know," he said haughtily, "the town has given the Society jurisdiction over this wonderful old building, and therefore, I'm the proper person to take possession of the gold for the time being."

"I've never heard such a truck load of bull," Connor said. "I'm calling the police." He picked up the phone and began to dial.

"Do you really think the police will be-lieve a crazy man like you?" Chang asked. "I bring real value to this town and all you do is paint stupid pictures no one wants."

"Now, wait a minute," Worthington said, but Chang wasn't waiting. He lunged at Jupiter.

In his surprise, Jupiter pushed out his hands to fend off the attack, and Chang snatched the envelope, wrenching it from Jupiter's fingers. Unprepared for the move, Jupiter almost fell as he tried to grab the envelope back.

"Let's get out of here," John Chang said.

Chang and his henchman had come quite far into Connor's studio, and as they had, Mallory had moved behind them. Now, in the scuffle that ensued, she shoved the chair on casters across the floor. It skidded sideways and clipped Chang's companion behind the knees. He lost his balance and fell, dropping the pipe – which Mallory swiftly picked up.

As Chang hesitated for a moment, Pete launched himself through the air and tackled the man, and they both fell to the floor with a sickening crash. Chang got the worst of it because he was underneath. Pete was on his feet in no time, towering over Chang, holding the pouch he had wrested away from him. Mallory moved closer with the pipe.

"Nice work!" Connor said admiringly. "The police are on the way! Do you play football?"

"Soccer," Pete said. "Football, if you live in Italy."

Chang staggered to his feet and was moving to get away.

"Hold them!" Worthington said. But before anyone could do anything, Chang and his knife-scarred accomplice were gone.

"Don't worry," Jupiter said. "The police will easily find them."

Two policemen arrived in no time, their siren screaming. It took a while to explain everything that had happened. The two men listened carefully, and then the sergeant said that he'd better take possession of the gold for the time being.

"All right," Jupiter said reluctantly, "but since it doesn't belong to any of us, I'd like a receipt, made out to Isabella Chang, care of The Three Investigators. Before you do that, I think we should find a scale and weigh the pouch. As you know, with gold, even a small difference in weight affects the value significantly."

"I've got a digital paint mixing scale," Connor said. He dragged it out of a corner and set it on the table. Jupiter put the leather envelope on it, and everyone gasped when the numbers settled at almost four hundred ounces – close to twenty-five pounds.

The police gave Jupiter the receipt – made out, as Jupiter had asked, to Isabella Chang, and care of the firm. Jupiter gave them Isabella Chang's address and telephone number, and also a Three Investigators card.

"If I need anything further from you," the sergeant said, "I presume I can call you at the Headquarters for your firm?"

"In a few days," Jupiter said. "In the meantime, please call Bob Andrews's cellphone number if it's urgent."

After the police left, the six of them walked out of the old Carnegie Library together, past the place where the stacks of books had stood. The card catalogue was no longer there, or the circulation desk, or the reading tables. But all of them were there in Jupiter's imagination.

At one of the tables a young Chinese man sat, intent on the book he was reading. Though he sat in Auburn, California, his mind was very far away, sailing distant seas.

"Isabella Chang was right!" Pete said as they all stood blinking in the sunlight on the front steps.

"Her faith in us was not entirely misplaced," Jupiter said. "Still, we would never have succeeded so quickly if it hadn't been for Mallory's remarkable memory − and the happy accident of meeting her at The Next Chapter Bookstore. Without her, we might never have succeeded at all."

"And she really helped out when she pushed that chair!" Pete said. "What are we going to do with all the money? Time to start planning our next vacation!"

"Let's not get carried away," Jupiter said. "Hector Sebastian was good enough to bankroll us, so we ought to pay him back."

"But that was a present!" Pete said.

"Nevertheless," Jupiter said. "Remember that the reason we took this case had nothing to do with money. That has never been what we were interested in. Whatever reward Ms. Chang offers, we will need to think about it carefully and spend it wisely, for our good and the good of The Three Investigators."

He looked at Worthington thoughtfully.

"I don't know what the reward will be," Jupiter said, "but it could be substantial. Perhaps it might be enough for us to purchase a secondhand car − even enough for us to pay

Worthington to drive us around for a while."

Worthington smiled broadly. "I hardly know what to say!"

"Just say yes!" Pete said. "Jeez, Jupe, what a genius idea."

"A *good* idea," Jupiter said. "You know I dislike the word 'genius.'" He did think it was a good idea, though. A very good idea, indeed.

As he and the others stood on the library steps − a library built with a generous grant from a very successful Scottish immigrant − Jupiter was thinking not only about Andrew Carnegie but also John Muir and Angus O'Malley and Li Chang's parents. All of them had come to California from somewhere very far away, and once they got here, all of them had changed the lives of those around them for the better.

In the case of Muir and Carnegie, they had done that on a very grand scale, and in the case of Angus O'Malley and Li Chang's father and mother, their influence had been smaller − though more intense to the people whose lives they had directly touched.

There really was something very special about America, just as Isabella Chang had suggested. Whoever they were, and whatever they wanted, when people came here, if they believed in themselves and worked hard, they could make a difference in the world.

Of course, luck had something to do with it, also, and this was a case where luck had broken their way any number of times.

When John Chang had pretended to compliment what he had called their "little enterprise" and had remarked that they had never failed to solve a mystery that had come to their attention, Jupiter had said that they were just three normal teenagers who'd had a lot of luck. At the time, Jupiter had been trying to lull John Chang into a false sense of security, but he now realized he'd been telling the truth anyway.

Not that they were three normal teenagers, of course, but that they'd had a lot of luck – and not just on this case, but long before it. For one thing, they'd had the luck to have both Worthington and Hector Sebastian take an interest in them, and help them; for another, they'd had the luck to be born into families that believed that young people should be permitted to make their own decisions and learn from their own mistakes. If their families hadn't trusted them with independence, they would never had gotten anywhere at all, Jupiter reflected.

As for the case they were just wrapping up, it was interesting to think it had started with Pete telling Bob that Uncle Titus had acquired a bunch of what Pete had called "old Chinese good luck charms." There was, of course, no such thing as either a curse *or* a good luck charm – at least not one that worked!

Still, it had to be admitted that the Talisman Against Demons, which was even now swaying in the wind in front of Aunt Mathilda's office, had proved to be good luck for The Three Investigators – and so had the fact that Mallory MacLeod had come into the yard, seen it, and remembered it so clearly later.

It had also been very lucky that The Three Investigators had been able to find out about John Chang's secret windowsill drawer before they got to his house. The fact was, luck was everywhere, and Jupiter had to start admitting it. Still, if you didn't work hard to begin with – if you didn't dedicate yourself to the tasks you undertook, and work until they were finished – luck wouldn't be the slightest use to you.

In fact, while it *was* important to remember that chance – or coincidence – played a role in every life, there was an old Latin proverb Jupiter was fond of which suggested that luck came to those who put themselves in its path to begin with. In the proverb, the word "luck" was replaced with the word "fortune" and people who went out and tried to do something in the world were called the "bold."

"Fortune favors the bold," Jupiter suddenly said aloud.

To his surprise, the others looked at him and cheered.

16

An Abecedarian Academy

Five days later, the boys were in Headquarters, wrapping up the case. They'd been glad to get back home to Rocky Beach and had spent the first three days with their families, and resting. They'd gotten a lot of things done on their trip, but sleep had not been one of them. Still, Bob, in particular, had had a lot to do when they got back, putting his notes in order. This was the first time he'd be writing up a case completely by himself, and he was determined to do the best job he possibly could.

On the drive back to southern California, he and Pete and Jupiter had talked a lot about the question of why Li Chang had hidden the gold to begin with — and why he hadn't told his wife where it was hidden. While they would probably never know the answer to this question — not for sure and certain, anyway — Bob felt that any future readers would expect a working hypothesis — and the date of Li Chang's Last Will and Testament had given him a place to start.

From his genealogical research, Bob

knew that Li Chang's mother, Rose, had died in early June of 1917, and since Li Chang's will was dated August of that same year, Li had only had the gold in his possession for two months when he hid it. By then, he was fifty-eight years old and had lived most of his life knowing his mother believed she had cursed the treasure.

Li himself hadn't believed in the curse, but even so, with only six years to go until it expired – and having also inherited a successful laundry and dry goods business – Li had probably felt that since he had lived his whole life happily without the gold, he should honor his mother by honoring her wishes concerning it.

However, Li had been human (like everyone else), and since he *didn't* believe in the curse, he might have been worried that if he kept the gold too close, the day might come when he would be tempted to take it out and use it. He might have thought it would be easier to control a sudden impulse if he put the leather envelope in a place from which it would be harder to recover it.

As to why he didn't tell his wife where he had hidden it but left her a puzzle she didn't seem well equipped to solve, the answer to *that* seemed a little harder. Bob had to assume Li Chang had never imagined he'd die before he retrieved the treasure and that he'd composed the cipher using the talisman and the book mainly because he loved puzzles.

In other words, Bob thought, he had done it mostly to amuse himself – not thinking he would be dying any time soon.

This seemed to Bob a workable hypothesis, but even if it was true in all particulars, it still seemed strange that Li hadn't trusted his wife with the information during his lifetime. Bob's mother and father knew everything important about one another's lives, and so did Pete's, Pete said.

The only thing Bob could think of to explain the fact that Li kept such crucial information from his wife was that he feared she might talk about it to one of her friends or neighbors – and then the secret would get out. Although that was sheer speculation, Pete and Jupiter had agreed that it was plausible, and now the three of them were in Headquarters, taking stock of all that had happened and waiting for a call from Isabella Chang.

On the desk in front of them was the gold assayer's scale that Gordon Small had discovered in his attic and had mounted on the wall of his café. It probably had belonged to Li Chang's father, and before they left Auburn, Gordon Small had given it to them as a memento.

"You deserve it, boys!" he had said. "And that miner standing in its middle makes it a curiosity as well as a memento!"

Since then, one very important thing had happened. They had heard about it from both Connor O'Malley and the police sergeant. John Chang had hired a lawyer and filed an emergency order asking the Auburn District Court to give him the gold for safekeeping – citing his leadership of the Gold Country Historical Society and also its written agreement with the city – but the judge had found this argument laughable.

In fact, he'd told John Chang he might recommend that the police look into charges of attempted robbery, or worse. The judge had also ruled that the piece of paper in the leather pouch constituted a legal and valid will, and on the recommendation of a town lawyer (who, by then, had done research on Li Chang's descendants, and also on Li Chang's handwriting), the judge had awarded the gold to Isabella Chang.

The boys had called her a second time

before they left Auburn to let her know that they had found the gold. She, of course, had been thrilled – but mostly, she said, because their discovery vindicated her belief in them. Now, they were about to talk with her again, and while they waited for 1:00 to roll around, they were discussing the case.

"I couldn't believe the way you tackled John Chang," Bob said to Pete. "That was awesome."

He reached across the scarred desk and bumped Pete's fist with his.

"After all we'd been through," Pete said, "there was no way he was getting away with Isabella Chang's gold!"

"I'll bet he has some bruises to remember you by," Jupiter said. "But getting down to business. This was a difficult case, because it began so matter-of-factly, and our expectations were constantly changing. After our first meeting with Isabella Chang, I thought most of the work would be done by Bob at the library and online. In fact, Ms. Chang might never have hired us if her eyesight had been better and she was able to use computers with ease."

"But right from the start," Bob said, "there were discrepancies in what I found. Ms. Chang, for example, thought Li Chang's father had been killed because of prejudice against the Chinese. But then I found that article where Rose Chang swore the killer *was* Chinese. I thought at first that maybe she'd been mistaken, or that the killer had disguised himself, but she was telling the truth."

"Except," Pete said, "he wasn't just Chinese. He was family. And the whole thing might have been an accident."

"If it hadn't been for the curse – which was another accident – everything might have turned out very differently," Jupiter said. "Perhaps Hao Chang would have gone after the gold again. Or perhaps Li's mother, or Li himself, would have spent it.

"I'm glad we came up with an explanation as to why Li hid the gold and then devised the book cipher and the map," Bob said.

"Yes," Jupiter said. "I'm sure he wanted his wife to have the gold. But as a boy, he'd loved puzzles, and at the time of his death, all his clues were together in one place. The book cipher was on one side of the talisman, the map on the other. And the book itself was right there in their house."

At that moment the phone rang, and Jupiter punched the speakerphone button.

"Three Investigators Headquarters," he

said.

"Jupiter, is that you? It's Isabella Chang. I couldn't wait 'til one o'clock. I just got a call from the bank that the gold has arrived in southern California. Of course, it hasn't been processed fully, and that will take some time. But all your work has come to fruition, and all of a sudden I'm a very rich woman."

"Gee, Ms. Chang," Pete said. "That's great."

"We loved the case," Bob said. "Thanks for having faith in us."

"I've lived modestly all my life," Isabella Chang said, "and I see no reason to change that now. Of course, I'll use some of the money to fix up my house and garden a bit, and I think I'll also use some of it to publish my book on one-room schoolhouses. I'd like to do that myself, rather than relying on someone else. But in the spirit of Andrew Carnegie, whose library meant so much to my ancestor, I'm going to give most of the rest of it away to worthy causes. And I wanted to start with The Three Investigators. As I told you when you were still in Auburn, I intend you to have ten percent of the money − as a finder's fee and as a reward for your most ingenious work."

"Ten per cent!" Pete shouted, as if he'd

just calculated this in his head. "Why that's – "

"A lot of money," Isabella Chang said. "And you deserve every penny. But please remember that I never believed in the gold, and finding it was not the reason I hired you. I wanted information about Li Chang, and what you have given to me is beyond anything I could have hoped for. Before you took the case, he was a shadowy figure in the distant past and now – well, let me just say he's more real to me than most of the people I see every day. Bob, I can't thank you enough for the photograph of the plaque he made when he graduated from eighth grade. And I'm going to frame the copy you boys made for me of the book cipher and the map, together with Li's *Last Will and Testament*.

"His whole life is real to me – I can imagine him the night his father met such an untimely end, and at his desk in Angus O'Malley's school. I imagine him sending secret messages to his young friend, and making his plaque, and moving to Auburn with his mother. Everything. Working at the laundry and the library, hiding the gold – "

"I'm very glad, Jupiter said. "We're very glad to have been able to help you."

"Now I want you all to come visit me

soon. I want to have you over to my house for a celebratory dinner, so please check with your parents and call me back when you've found a date."

"Thanks, Ms. Chang," Pete said. "We will."

"If you talk with Hector Sebastian," Jupiter added, "please tell him we'd like to return the seed money he gave us for our trip."

They all said their goodbyes and when Jupiter punched the button to hang up the phone, they all sat back in disbelief.

Before Bob could think of what to say, Jupiter was talking.

"I had a hunch," he said, "that Ms. Chang was not the sort of person to go back on a spoken promise, and that we might have a windfall on our hands, so I pondered what to do with it. I have a proposition. Please listen carefully before you say anything." He opened the drawer of the desk and took out five large black document clips.

"Now this pile of document clips," he said, "represents the money we'll get. I propose we divide it into five equal parts." He separated the document clips on the desktop. "We all have college funds," he said, "so I propose that three of the five parts go to those − one for each of us." He pushed a document clip toward Pete, one toward Bob, and one toward himself. "That leaves two parts."

He picked up a document clip and stared at it. "As I suggested the day we found the gold, if the reward proved to be substantial, it might be enough for us to purchase a second-hand car and to pay Worthington to drive us around in it. I therefore propose we use one part to buy a used car. We can register it in my uncle's name. I also propose we open a savings account in the firm's name and put the last of the money there. We can use it for whatever might come up, including hiring Worthington to drive us around when we need him to."

"Wow!" Pete said. "You think of every-thing!"

Bob was impressed. Jupiter's plan was both simple and judicious, and he and Pete readily and enthusiastically agreed. Pete picked up the document clip representing the car and pushed it around the table, vroom-vroom-vrooming.

Bob laughed.

"Only kidding," Pete said.

Jupiter opened the drawer and swept the document clips back inside.

"There's one other thing," Bob said.

"Since we're talking about money – or at least about the part that's going in the bank – I think we should use some of that to get a thank-you present for Mallory MacLeod. If it hadn't been for her, we might never have found the gold at all."

"Absolutely correct," Jupiter said. "And very good of you to think of it, Bob."

"No arguments from me," Pete said.

"Bob," Jupiter said. "I have a hunch you have an idea for an appropriate present."

"I do," Bob said. He reminded his friends about the painted wooden trunk that Mallory had admired at the bookstore in Grass Valley – the one with wrought-iron handles and a name and a date painted on the outside.

"It was an immigrant's trunk," he said. "And since she's just come over from Scotland, she's sort of an immigrant, too, isn't she? We know she likes handmade things. Things that are one of a kind. I took pictures of it when we were in the store, so we could have it made and painted just the way *that* one was – except, of course, it would be *her* name on the front, and the year she and her mother arrived in California. I think she'd really, really like it."

"So it would be a 'Welcome to America' present as well as a thank-you present," Pete said.

"Exactly," Bob agreed.

"But where would we get such a thing?" Jupiter asked.

"There's lots of reclaimed wood around the Salvage Yard," Bob said. "And Leif and Magnus are master carpenters. Maybe we could hire them to make a trunk for her. I mean, they're Norwegian and everything, and although she called the trunk Scandinavian, not Norwegian, there has to be a lot of crossover between different Scandinavian countries, don't you think?"

"That," Jupiter said, "is a first-class idea."

The boys went to find Uncle Titus and Aunt Mathilda − after which the five of them sought out Leif and Magnus in their workshop. The brothers said they'd love to build an immigrant's trunk, and that they even knew someone they thought could paint the outside when it was done. Bob said he would send them the pictures he'd taken of the model so they could see the way it was painted and constructed, and so they could match the wrought-iron handles and iron lock. The Salvage Yard was filled with old locks and keys, and somewhere or other it almost certainly had some old wrought-iron handles.

Bob rode his bike home from the Salvage Yard, pleased about his idea. Everything would take time, of course – getting the money, buying the car, having Leif and Magnus make the trunk. He was wondering whether Mallory would like it as much as he hoped she would when a series of honks from behind almost sent him careening onto the sidewalk. A red convertible sports car screeched to a stop. In the driver's seat was Skinny Norris wearing a porkpie hat. He looked so ridiculous Bob forgot about being startled and started laughing.

"What's so funny, Miss Andrews?" Skinny asked.

"Where'd you get the hat, Skinny?" Bob said. "You need to be cool to wear one of those."

"Never mind that," Skinny said. "Mally-Wally told me about your little adventure up north."

"Don't call her Mally-Wally," Bob said. "Her name is Mallory."

"Ho ho," Skinny said. "To *you*, maybe. Not to me. And what's all this about gold?"

"Me and Pete and Jupe are millionaires now," Bob said. "We're each going to have a little red sports car."

"You're not old enough to drive," Skinny said.

"No, but we will be in two years," Bob said. "And the only reason *you* can drive is because your license is out-of-state. So long, Skinny." He started pedaling away, then called back over his shoulder, "Say hello to Mallory, if you see her."

"Yeah, right," Skinny yelled. "Like in a million billion years. Anyway, she's spending all her time looking for a summer job. Her mother's back at work now."

He stepped on the gas and soon disappeared down the road. Bob wouldn't say he liked Skinny – not in a million billion years – but he could be fun to talk to sometimes. Bob wondered what kind of a job Mallory was looking for. Maybe he could help her find one.

That evening, after dinner, Bob took his laptop up to his room, set it on his desk, and then sat thinking of Hector Sebastian. Bob had written him an e-mail the day before, and Mr. Sebastian had written back to say that he'd arrived in Dubois, Wyoming, and to give Bob his number there. Bob now found himself dialing the number, for reasons he didn't really understand.

"Bob!" Hector Sebastian said when he

picked up. "How good to hear from you. I've talked to Isabella, and she's told me everything. What an adventure! She also mentioned something about your wanting to pay me back the money I gave you."

"Yes," Bob said, "since we have so much now – "

"I won't hear of such a thing. Under no conditions. I don't care if you're rich as Croesus. That money was a gift, and one doesn't return a gift. If you're lucky enough to have more than you need yourself, it's always satisfying to help other people get better at what they do."

Bob thought of Andrew Carnegie.

"I see what you mean," he said. He paused and took a deep breath. "How's the writing going?" he asked.

"The writing?" Hector Sebastian said. "Well, I'm still getting unpacked, so I really haven't started. But I have a number of ideas tumbling away upstairs. One of these days I'll sit down and see what happens. What about you?"

"Me?" Bob asked. He was surprised at how high his voice sounded.

"Didn't you call me – really – because you wanted to talk about writing up the case?"

"Well," Bob said. "I – "

"Bob," said Hector Sebastian. "I have every confidence in you. Your research is exhaustive and your sense of order impeccable. From what I have seen of your prose, you are developing into a fine writer. You have everything it will take to turn your experiences and those of your friends into compelling reading."

"Thank you," Bob said.

"You're welcome," said Hector Sebastian. "I have to go now, but I really hope we'll stay in touch. You don't ever need an excuse to call."

Bob ended the call and stared off into the distance again. He felt a good deal older than he had when he and Jupiter and Pete had left Rocky Beach for Yosemite, and he found himself remembering the morning when he and his parents had been eating breakfast and he'd smelled the smoke from Mr. Townsend's yard.

It was funny how that smoke from Rocky Beach was bound up in his mind with the moment in Auburn when John Chang and his henchman had suddenly left the house on Aeolia Drive, filled with irrational fears. They hadn't been obvious bad guys, and if the judge had been less able to see John Chang for who he really was, Chang might have won.

Bob found himself thinking about all the people they had ended up meeting on their trip to the Gold Country – not just John Chang and the man with the knife scar, but Randy at the Sighing Pines Campground and Cabins, the squatter with the shotgun, the woman at the museum, the owner of the bookstore, Gordon Small, Connor O'Malley – and realizing he was going to need to make them characters in his story about what had happened.

Mallory, too, would need to be made into a character of sorts, and although he had found himself saying to her at the bookstore that because Li Chang's mother was Irish and his father was Chinese, he had started to identify with him a little, he actually identified with Mallory even more. She was so distinctively *herself*, he thought, and it had been so interesting to see her meeting Jupiter for the first time.

As for what he had told Mallory about Li Chang, although it was true, it would also have been true if Li Chang had been half Russian and half Italian. What Bob had meant was that having parents from two different countries gave you a feeling of disjointedness from time to time.

In Bob's life, that feeling had mostly arisen when people assumed he knew about

China just because one of his two sets of grandparents had been born there. But not only did he not know all that much about the country they had come from – fleeing for their lives – since they had died in their early 60s, in San Francisco, and since his mother didn't talk about them much, Bob knew almost nothing about them.

Although he felt a lot more connected to the other side of his family – and loved the idea that he and Mallory might have a common ancestor! – when he had read a book about the Viking attacks on Britain, he'd been freaked out by the blood-soaked nature of their warfare. In fact, although he found all history fascinating, he couldn't exactly see himself participating in the activities of *either* of his sets of ancestors.

Not that that was all that surprising, when you came right down to it. A human being was one of a kind, after all. Like a mortised timber pulled out of an old barn and used as a joist in a library. Like a handmade immigrant's trunk. Like the most interesting objects Jupiter's Uncle Titus brought back to the Salvage Yard.

People were individuals first and foremost, Bob thought with real satisfaction. Before they were boys or girls or Scottish or Irish or Welsh or Mexican or Chinese – before they were painters or café owners or real estate developers – they were simply who they were. And every one of them, as it turned out – and whether they realized it or not – was a student in a gigantic one-room schoolhouse where being curious was a tremendous asset and investigating everything that came your way would always stand you in good stead.

Bob turned back to his laptop, opened a file, labeled it *The Mystery of The Abecedarian Academy*, took a deep breath, and began to type.

ABOUT THE AUTHORS

Elizabeth Arthur

Elizabeth was born on November 15, 1953 in New York City. She is the daughter of Robert Arthur, the creator of The Three Investigators series. She was educated at Concord Academy in Concord, Massachusetts, the University of Michigan in Ann Arbor, Michigan, Notre Dame University of Nelson, British Columbia, and the University of Victoria in Victoria, British Columbia.

Before she started working on the New Three Investigators series in December of 2018, Elizabeth spent most of her life writing for adults. *Island Sojourn* – a memoir about building a house on a wilderness island in northern Canada – was published in 1980 by Harper and Row. A second memoir, *Looking For The Klondike Stone*, was published by Knopf in 1992. She is also the author of the novels *Beyond the Mountain, Bad Guys, Binding Spell, Antarctic Navigation,* and *Bring Deeps.*

Elizabeth's writing has received fellowships, grants, and awards from the Bread Loaf Writer's Conference, the Ossabaw Island Project, the Vermont Council on the Arts, and the Indiana Arts Commission. She twice received fellowships from the National Endowment for the Arts and was the first novelist ever given an Antarctic Artists and Writers Operational Support Grant from the National Science Foundation.

Her novel *Antarctic Navigation* was chosen by the New York *Times* as a Notable Book, received a Critics' Choice Award from the San Francisco *Review of Books*, and was chosen as a Best Book of 1995 by *A Common Reader*. In 1996 the novel received the Ohioana Book Award for Fiction from the Ohioana Library Association.

Elizabeth has also taught creative writing at Miami University in Oxford, Ohio; the University of Cincinnati; and Indiana University/Purdue University of Indianapolis, where she directed the creative writing program. She and Steven Bauer met in 1980 at the Bread Loaf Writer's Conference and have been married since June of 1982.

Steven Bauer

Steven was born on September 10, 1948 in Newark, New Jersey. He was educated at Hanover Park High School in East Hanover, New Jersey, Trinity College in Hartford, Connecticut, and the University of Massachusetts in Amherst, Massachusetts. In 1970 he received a B.A. with Honors in English from Trinity, and in 1975 he received an M.F.A. in English from the University of Massachusetts.

Steven is the author of three books for young people – *Satyrday*, 1980; *The Strange and Wonderful Tale of Robert McDoodle*, 1999; and *A Cat of a Different Color*, 2000. His book of poems *Daylight Savings* was published by Gibbs Smith in 1989 and won the Peregrine Smith Poetry Prize.

Steven's work has received fellowships from the Bread Loaf Writer's Conference and the Fine Arts Work Center in Provincetown, Massachusetts. In addition, he has been given grants and awards from the American Library Association, the Parents' Choice Foundation, the Ossabaw Island Project, the Massachusetts Arts Council, and the Indiana Arts Commission.

From 1979 to 1982, Steven taught literature and creative writing at Colby College in Waterville, Maine. From 1982 to 2009 he taught at Miami University in Oxford, Ohio where he directed the graduate and undergraduate creative writing programs. In 2010 he established Hollow Tree Literary Services, an independent editing business.